"Not another one."

Casey looked at Matt Reilly—the rancher who lived next door. "Another what?"

"Do-gooder," he groaned. "You people create more problems than you solve."

Stung, she retorted, "I'm an artist, not an environmentalist, Mr. Reilly." She saw her new neighbor glance at the stack of canvases that leaned against the wall. "Is there something else you wanted?" she asked, hoping to forestall any more questions.

"Yes. I want to buy you out. Your strip of property would—"

"I'm sorry. There's no question of my selling." She stood in a gesture of dismissal. "Now, if that's all you have to say, I'll ask you to leave. I'm—"

"That's not all by a long shot. A city girl like you won't survive out here on the prairie. You'll never make it."

Casey bristled visibly. "I'll do whatever I have to. Now if you'll excuse me..." She motioned toward the door.

"All right, I'll go. But don't think I won't be back."

Alina Roberts is a native of Washington, D.C., but after having lived in Colorado for eighteen years, she now considers it her home—although she does admit that the winters there are a bit too long! Stories by Alina have appeared in many magazines, and *Prairie Summer* is her second published novel. The incidents described in the book are based on actual events.

To all my friends at
Colorado Romance Writers.
Together we can.

PRAIRIE SUMMER

Alina Roberts

W♦RLDWIDE.

TORONTO • NEW YORK • LONDON
AMSTERDAM • PARIS • SYDNEY • HAMBURG
STOCKHOLM • ATHENS • TOKYO • MILAN
MADRID • WARSAW • BUDAPEST • AUCKLAND

Special thanks and acknowledgment to
Jane Choate

ISBN 0-373-83274-5

PRAIRIE SUMMER

One

Nearly doubled over, Casey wrestled with the trunk, trying to hoist it out of the car. With her neighbor's help last night, putting it in had not been that difficult. Now, however, she couldn't lift it by herself. She would have to unpack part of it, she decided unwillingly, making several trips, instead of one. Having already unloaded the other luggage, she was anxious to finish.

Dusk had settled, softening the rough edges of the Colorado landscape with a lavender haze. She paused for a moment, absorbing the harsh beauty of the land. It wasn't an easy kind of beauty, but the kind that demanded a response.

A deep voice, coming from behind her, startled her. "Let me help you with that."

Casey swung around to face a tall—he must have been well over six feet—commanding figure. She let her eyes travel upward until she encountered a pair of startling blue eyes set in a deeply tanned face.

She flushed. Fear made her voice sharp. "You startled me."

"Sorry." A smile touched his mouth briefly. "I'd like to see the new owner. A Mr. K. C. Allen."

"I'm K. C. Allen," she said, and enjoyed the surprise in his eyes. "Katherine Colleen Allen. Casey for short. Now that you know my name, who are you?"

"Matt Reilly. We're neighbors."

She took the hand he offered. Calluses rasped against her palm. She turned back to the trunk.

Large hands gripped her arms and firmly set her aside. With no visible effort, he hefted the trunk onto his shoulders and started toward the house.

"Where do you want this?" he called.

"Just inside the door." She ran in front of him to open it. "Thanks. I couldn't have managed on my own."

Depositing the trunk to one side, he looked about. "I see old Zach left a few things."

Casey nodded. The house was partially furnished. A rocking chair and an uncomfortable-looking couch occupied most of the small living room. A round table and two folding chairs filled the small kitchen. She smiled, remembering the old-fashioned trundle bed in the only bedroom, which her son, Robbie, now occupied.

"Did you know Mr. Morrow?" she asked at last.

"Everyone knew Zachary Morrow. He's practically a legend around here," Matt said. "Just before he died, he asked me to give this to the new owner." He laughed briefly. "At the time, I had no idea it would be ..."

He handed her a sealed envelope. Casey fingered it curiously, eager to see its contents but reluctant to open it in front of a stranger.

"Yeah, Zach was a real character," Matt continued. "He prided himself on being eccentric."

"How so?"

Matt waved a hand about. "His near-poverty existence, when it wasn't necessary. His shutting himself off from the rest of the world, except for a few friends. His dogged determination to hold on to this piece of land, even though he couldn't take care of it. His insistence that the prairie dogs be left alone."

"He was within his rights," she defended her benefactor, remembering the instructions from Zach's lawyer that she was to continue letting the prairie dogs make their home on the land. "As for protecting the prairie dogs, I think he deserved to be commended, not condemned."

"Of course he was within his rights," Matt agreed impatiently, "but it made it hard on his friends who wanted to help him. And those prairie dogs cost his neighbors a bundle of money, not to mention a pack of trouble."

"Perhaps he thought that help might cost him his independence and freedom," Casey countered. For some perverse reason, she wanted to needle this man, who gave the impression of too often having everything his own way. "And I'm afraid I have to side with Mr. Morrow about the animals."

"Not another one," he muttered.

"Another what?"

"Save us from the world's do-gooders," he groaned. "You people create more problems than you solve."

Stung, she retorted, "I'm an artist, not an environmentalist, Mr. Reilly." She saw him glance at the stack of canvases that leaned against the wall.

"You're not here by yourself, are you?" he asked.

"No," she said quietly. "I have a six-year-old son. It was a long trip, and he's already asleep. Is there anything else?" Her voice betrayed her exhaustion, and she struggled to keep it steady.

"Yes, I want to buy you out. Your strip of property would—"

"I'm sorry. There's no question of my selling. We intend to make our home here." She stood in a gesture of dismissal. "Now, if that's all you have to say, I'm very tired, and I still have a lot to do."

"That's not all by a long shot. You can't live here. You and a child alone."

"I'll do whatever I have to."

During the two years since Dave's death, she'd had to struggle to remain independent. Though they couldn't af-

ford it, Dave's parents had offered to help out. She'd refused, determined to make it on her own. And she had.
She wasn't about to give that up now. "If you'll excuse
me." She looked pointedly at the door.

"It's late," he said. "But I'll be back. You don't understand what you're taking on."

She didn't trust herself to answer that.

"Till tomorrow then." He slammed the door behind
him.

Casey stared after him, startled more by her reaction to
him than by anything he'd said.

Odd that a total stranger should affect her so strongly.
Of course, she had nothing to fear from him. The house
and land were hers. No one could force her to sell against
her wishes. Resolutely she put Matt Reilly out of her mind.

The letter, forgotten during her confrontation with
Matt, now beckoned to her. Ripping it open, she stared at
it.

Dear Katherine,
I was sorry to hear of your mother's death. I've
known her since her birth. She was very special to me.
I'd hoped that you and I would meet one day, but that
now appears impossible. Please accept this gift in
memory of her. As you know, I let the prairie dogs
make their home on this land. I've done it all my life
and have never regretted it. Please take care of them.
                                         Sincerely,
                                         Zach Morrow

Tears shimmered in Casey's eyes as she read the letter
once more, pausing over the mention of her mother. How
she wished she'd known Zach Morrow. She was sure she
would have liked him.

He'd left her with a charge, and she intended to honor
it. Wiping the last smudges of tears away, she looked

around, trying to understand the man who'd lived here for more than fifty years.

Neglect and time had taken their toll on the house and its furnishings. Dust coated not only the sparse pieces of furniture but seemed to be embedded into their surfaces.

Obviously Zach Morrow had spent little time inside. Perhaps she would find the answer outdoors. Despite her exhaustion, she wandered outside, looking for clues to the character of her mother's godfather.

Red and purple streaked the summer sky, providing an impressive backdrop for the craggy peaks of the Rockies. Clumps of grass dotted the ground. A cacophony of sound greeted her as a flock of sparrows gathered in the huge cottonwood trees that shaded the house. A smile erased the tiredness from her face as she listened to their chatter.

"So this is what you're about, Zach," she said. "I won't let you down."

Inside once more, she felt her smile vanish as she looked about at the shabby interior of what was now her and Robbie's home. Her head reeled with all that had to be done. Chipped green enamel on the kitchen cabinets showed glimpses of what might have been lovely hardwood beneath. Uncovering it would require hours of tedious stripping and sanding. The oak plank floor, too, would need refinishing. Suddenly she smiled. *One step at a time*. Her mother's words repeated themselves in her mind as they had so often in the past. *Not everything can be done at once,* her mother would say to the young impulsive Casey whose impatience often led her to tackle more than was reasonable. Or more than she could handle alone. Never one to refuse to try anything, Casey often leapt before she looked.

This time, though, she faced a very real limitation—money. Or the lack thereof, she amended wryly. Two thousand dollars was all that remained of selling everything to pay off Dave's medical bills. The small amount from his life insurance had to be kept in reserve.

She and Dave had married straight out of college. They'd planned to set the world on fire, she with her art and Dave by opening his own computer-software business. She postponed her dream of illustrating children's books and took a job as a commercial artist to help with the bills until his business was rolling.

Four year later, just when his business *had* started to pick up considerably, Dave had developed a brain tumor that left him too ill to work. As the disease progressed, she left her job to care for him. When he died, she struggled to make a living for Robbie and herself, once again shelving her dream. She'd learned something since Dave's death— she was a survivor.

Characteristically, Casey refused to feel sorry for herself. Now, with this mortgage-free house, they would have no worries about rent. She had noticed the good-size garden plot; perhaps next summer she could supplement their food budget by raising vegetables. She added that to her list of things to do—find out what grows well here.

The first order of business would be to give the house a thorough cleaning. A minimum of unpacking, though, was all she could manage now.

Sponging off in the shower in the closet-size bathroom, she realized how primitive the plumbing was and prayed it would hold out. The pressure was feeble at best, and pipes sputtered ominously in protest against their unaccustomed use.

Dressed in thin cotton pajamas, she slipped gratefully beneath the sheets. Even the lumpy mattress felt good. What a blessing Mr. Morrow had an old-fashioned trundle bed that she and Robbie could both use. Someday she would add another bedroom. Until then, they'd have to make do with what was there. The gentle cadence of Robbie's soft steady breathing lulled her to sleep.

The next morning, she rubbed her eyes crossly. Matt Reilly had plagued her dreams, taunting her in them, just as he'd done the night before.

Her expression automatically softened as she gazed down at Robbie. Impossibly long red-gold eyelashes fanned lightly freckled cheeks; one small hand gripped a much-loved toy unicorn while the other formed a dimpled fist, pushed up against his chin.

Her marriage to Dave had been achingly brief, but she'd never regretted their time together. And he'd left her a precious legacy—Robbie. Careful not to wake the little boy, Casey stepped gingerly over the lower bed and slipped into a short robe. A quick shower—she dared not strain the capacities of the hot-water heater with its low water pressure—and fresh clothing saw her ready for the day. Padding out to the kitchen, she surveyed the remainder of the groceries they'd bought early yesterday morning—a third of a loaf of bread, two bananas and half a quart of milk. Breakfast would deplete their meager supplies. She added grocery shopping to her list of things to do.

"Mom, where are you?"

"Right here, honey," she answered, hurrying back into the bedroom. "Hey, sleepyhead. I thought you were going to be the first one up and out exploring this morning."

"Is it too late?"

"No, sweetheart, it's not late at all." She tugged on the tail of his pajama top. "Come on and help me put this bed back together."

Why is it things slide out so much more easily than they slide back in? she wondered in exasperation. After trying for the third time to make the latch work, she finally plopped down on the bed, pulling Robbie with her.

"We may just have to leave it this way." She pulled a comic face at him, ignoring the knock at the door as she surveyed the bed.

"It seems I've found you struggling with inanimate objects again," an amused voice said from the doorway. Casey stood and faced the man who had so disturbed her sleep last night. "Do you always walk into other people's homes uninvited?"

"Only when my knocks go unheeded. I *did* call out several times. Can I help?"

"We were trying to put this thing—" she pointed to the bed "—back together, but it won't budge."

"Let me take a look." He maneuvered the sliding mechanism and, within seconds, had the trundle bed back in place.

"Thanks."

"You're welcome." He turned to Robbie. "Hi. What's your name?"

"Robbie. I'm six years old, and I go to school."

"Glad to meet you, Robbie. I'm Matt."

"How old are you, Matt?"

Casey intervened hastily. "Robbie, that's none of our business. Why don't you go get washed and dressed?"

"That's all right," Matt said easily. "I'm thirty-four, Rob. A bit older than you."

Snatching some clean clothes from the stack on the floor, Casey bundled them and her son into the bathroom.

"We can talk out here," she said, indicating the living room.

Following her out of the room, he looked at the sagging sofa and then leaned against the wall. "You said last night you and your son were alone."

She nodded.

"Your husband?"

"He died two years ago."

She tried not to notice the compassion in Matt's eyes. She didn't need that. All she wanted was a chance to make a new life for herself and her son—on her own.

"I can't give up this place," she said, anticipating Matt's next words.

Robbie wandered into the living room. "I'm hungry."

"We'll have breakfast in just a minute. We'll eat picnic-style, okay?"

"Okay!"

Casey felt Matt's gaze on her and wondered what he was thinking. Probably deciding how to convince her to sell her property.

His next words confirmed it. "I'll leave you to your breakfast. But I'll be back. You don't know what you've taken on." And with that, he left.

Robbie was standing at the window. "Look." He pointed to the gray gelding that Matt mounted. "Isn't he wonderful?" he asked. Casey didn't know if he meant the horse or its rider.

"It's a beautiful horse," she agreed, preferring to think that Robbie's enthusiasm was directed there. "We'll probably see a lot of horses here."

"Could I have a pony? Please. I'd take such good care of it."

"You know I'd get you one if I could. There just isn't a way right now." Seeing his disappointed look, she added, "Maybe if I can get a job or sell some of my paintings, well, just maybe, we could swing a pony later on."

Robbie appeared content with that, accepting her half promise with touching faith. It was dangerous letting him believe that she could do anything. She'd tried to point out that there were some things she couldn't do, but Robbie refused to believe that.

A lump formed in her throat as she watched him. A fierce love swelled up within her, making her want to hold him close, to know he was safe and secure. After Dave's death, her instincts to overprotect came all too easily. She had to fight against smothering Robbie.

TWO

Every cow they passed, grazing on the seemingly endless range, elicited a delighted response from Robbie as Casey drove to the town of Little Falls. He swung his head back and forth, so as to not miss anything.

"Look, Mom! What are those little hills?" He pointed to a cluster of small mounds.

She followed the direction of his finger. "Prairie-dog holes. Prairie dogs tunnel underground and make their homes there. We'll see a lot more of them while we're here."

Casey relaxed and enjoyed the countryside, a palette of summer pastels. The sun cast a silvery edge over the heat-cured prairie grass. How she would like to paint it—a graceful windmill, a weathered barn, a pond shimmering in the sunshine. She listed the colors she would need for such a scene—burnt sienna, ocher—then laughed at herself. Here she was planning a painting when she had a hundred more important things to do.

Little Falls came as a pleasant surprise. Cottonwoods and aspens shaded wide streets; petunia-filled planters punctuated the street corners. A small park occupied the center of town. A family town, she decided approvingly. A place to build a home and raise a family. She easily located the elementary school—she'd learned that school started in four days—and registered Robbie in the first grade. A trip to the library netted a stack of books on gardening, plus a smaller number dealing with local wildlife. She'd have liked to browse longer, but Robbie's impatient glances toward the door persuaded her to postpone further reading.

On their way to the grocery store, they received several friendly nods. Casey gave shy smiles in return, while Robbie kept up a constant stream of chatter and questions. With careful shopping, she managed to buy what they needed and still keep within her budget.

While checking out, she spied Matt Reilly's tall figure striding across the street. Balancing a big sack of groceries in each arm, she urged Robbie, who was ogling a candy display, out of the store. As they headed toward the car, she shifted the bags slightly to ease the ache in her arms. The distance to the school, where she'd parked, was farther than she remembered. Robbie skipped happily beside her, intent on his game of not stepping on any lines in the pavement.

"Step on a crack, break your mother's back," he chanted.

Just as she decided the heavy sacks might indeed break her back, a familiar voice called to her.

"Mrs. Allen, it appears I'm destined to be your white knight," Matt said as he caught up to her. Without her quite knowing how, he relieved her of her groceries.

"I can manage," she said coolly, thinking that white knight was not how she regarded him at all.

"Are you always so gracious, or am I the only one who merits such treatment?"

She blushed guiltily, knowing she deserved that. "Thanks for your help," she managed at last. "Those sacks were heavier than I realized." She smiled in an effort to be more friendly.

He stowed the groceries into the back seat of the car. "I'm glad I ran into you. I wanted to apologize. I'm afraid I wasn't very neighborly last night or this morning."

"That's all right. You were disappointed about the land."

"I admit I'd like to buy your land, but that was no reason for me to snap at you like I did."

She extended her hand to find it covered by a much larger one. "Apology accepted if you'll accept mine. I'm sorry I overreacted."

"I'd like to talk to you about your land," he said. "Perhaps we could have dinner together. Tonight?"

Casey felt a keen stab of disappointment. He hadn't been trying to be friendly, after all. He still wanted her land. He was just trying another approach.

"No, thank you," she said stiffly. "Sorry to disappoint you, but my property is still not for sale."

"I didn't mean—"

"I know what you meant."

"There's something else," he said.

She eyed him suspiciously. "What?"

"The condition of your fences. If my cattle come to harm on your property, you'll be responsible." He paused. "Look, I'd like to help."

"Help who? Yourself or me?"

"You," he said, obviously curbing his impatience. "You can't string fence by yourself."

"Why not?"

"Independence is fine for those who can afford it. Just make sure you can," he said, clearly annoyed. "*My* fences are in order. *Yours* aren't." With that, he turned on his heel and strode off.

Casey glared after him.

"One more stop," she announced to Robbie who'd been checking out a squirrel scampering up a tree. "The hardware store."

Finding the store proved easier than determining what she needed for repairing fences. Finally she approached the young clerk and explained her problem.

"Kyle Bridges, ma'am," he introduced himself.

"Casey Allen."

Kyle showed her the reels of barbed wire and wire cutters. When she asked how to use them, he looked at her in amazement. "*You're* not going to put it up, are you?"

"I certainly am." Realizing he was not to blame for her problem, she apologized for her harsh-sounding reply. "Could you ring this up, please?"

Paying for the wire and tools left a big hole in her cash. But all she could hear was Matt Reilly's voice, challenging her independence.

The next day, while Robbie was busy exploring the property around the house, Casey wearily pushed a strand of hair back from her forehead. Taut muscles groaned in protest as she heaved yet another spool of wire. Though she wore leather gloves, she was careful to grip only the wire, avoiding the barbs spaced along it. She knew how easily they could bite into and tear soft flesh with only the briefest contact. Her left palm was still sore where she'd inadvertently caught it against one of the barbs.

Staggering with fatigue, she half-carried, half-dragged the spool of wire to the next fence post. Unwinding a long section, she started to tack the wire to the post. When she paused to push back her hair she saw Matt dismounting from his horse.

He covered the distance between them in a few long strides, then leaned against a post and watched.

Irritated at having him see her hot and disheveled, she dropped the wire cutters. As she stooped to pick them up, she found him standing over her.

"That wire wouldn't keep out a sick kitten, much less a fifteen-hundred-pound cow," he said.

She ignored him and tried to pull the wire taut. It persisted in remaining slack. Annoyed, she turned away. Taking a metal staple from her pocket, she started to hammer it to the post. His nearness made her clumsy, causing her to drop the hammer this time. Their hands touched as they both bent over at the same moment to retrieve it. Even through her leather gloves, she imagined she could feel the warmth of his fingers. She drew her hand away swiftly, afraid he might sense her reaction.

She finished securing the wire to the post and started toward the next one. Despite her best efforts, the wire still sagged when she attempted to tack it to the second post.

Matt followed her. "Wire should be tacked to the far post and then to the first one so that it can be pulled tight."

Exhaustion and his presence combined to make her even clumsier. Tugging at the wire with all her strength, she didn't watch her footing and caught one boot in the coil of wire on the ground. She lost her balance and toppled over backward.

Matt stood looming over her, concern mixed with amusement on his face. *If he dares laugh,* Casey vowed silently, *I'll...*

Her thought went unfinished as he reached out a hand to help her up. She glared at him, irrationally feeling it was his fault she'd fallen. She stared at the outstretched hand, tempted to ignore it.

Common sense battled with defiance and won. She accepted his hand and was immediately, if not gently, hauled up against a hard chest. She felt at home there in his arms, pressed against him. Aghast at the direction of her thoughts, she pushed away. She was freed, not, she guessed, through any efforts of her own, but because he had decided to release her.

"Thanks," she muttered.

He quirked an eyebrow at her less than gracious tone but said nothing. Instead, he shrugged off his leather vest and began unbuttoning his shirt, then tossed them both to the ground.

"What... what're you doing?" she stammered, disturbed by the sight of his bronzed chest, matted with light brown hair.

"Finishing this string of wire."

"It's my problem, and I'll handle it." She kept her eyes fastened on the brown column of his neck, refusing to meet his gaze.

"Like you just did?"

"Okay," she agreed reluctantly. If he were determined to help, she might as well take advantage of it and learn from him. "What should I do, boss?"

Matt spared her a moment's glance, indicating he wasn't deceived by her show of meekness. "Make some lemonade." He tweaked her nose. "And you might wipe that smudge of dirt off your nose."

Aware of just how grimy she must appear, she flushed. Her hair curled about her head in a riot of red and gold; sweat, mixed with dust, streaked her face. Her clothes were coated with dirt and wet with perspiration.

But she wasn't leaving yet. Not until she'd watched him string the wire. If she was going to make a home here, she had to know how to take care of the land, as well as the house. She studied the way he stretched the wire, how he positioned the metal staples.

After several minutes, Matt picked up his shirt and wiped his face. "I thought you were making lemonade," he reminded her.

"I'm going to." Conscious of his scrutiny, she walked toward the house. From behind her came the sound of soft laughter. She steeled herself not to turn around. She took a quick look in the backyard and noticed Robbie playing happily with the Lego set his grandparents had given him for his sixth birthday. So much for exploring, she thought wryly. Once inside the house and the safety of the bedroom, she peeled off her clothes, snatched up clean ones and marched into the bathroom.

Praying that the temperamental plumbing would behave, she turned on the shower and was relieved to find a tepid, if not hot spray. She scrubbed herself quickly and shampooed her hair, then let the water soothe her aching muscles. The stiffness eased somewhat and, regretfully, she turned off the water, knowing it would soon turn cold. She rubbed herself dry and slipped on the fresh clothes. Feeling more equipped to face the irritating Matt Reilly, she squared her shoulders and headed into the kitchen.

In a few minutes, she'd made the lemonade, set the pitcher and two glasses on a tray and carried it outside to the porch.

Matt joined her. She was relieved to see he'd put his shirt back on, though it remained unbuttoned.

"That section is finished," he said.

"Thanks." It seemed she was thanking him for something every other minute. But that was going to change. She would learn how to string fence, take care of the land and anything else that meant making a home for herself and Robbie.

"There's still a lot to be done. Zach let the whole place go—" he glanced around "—inside and out. Your work would be a lot easier without the tunnels caused by the prairie dogs. It weakens the ground so much the fence posts can't be driven in straight."

Frowning, she thought it over. "Can't I place the posts around the mounds?"

"Not and have them evenly spaced."

"Well, I'll just have to do the best I can, won't I?"

"Look, Casey, I know you like prairie dogs. All city folk think they're cute furry little creatures. What they don't realize is the damage they do to the land. It's not just the ranchers who don't like them. They destroy crops, too."

"So the farmers don't like them, either?"

"You got it." He finished buttoning his shirt. "Aside from everything else, they're competitors for the food. Did you know that thirty-two prairie dogs forage as much as one sheep? Two hundred and fifty can eat as much as a cow. In a drought, with every blade of grass worth more than gold, that can be disastrous. Not only to the ranchers, but to all those who depend upon them."

"But I can't just destroy them!"

"*You* wouldn't have to do it."

She recoiled in distaste at his implication. "I think we'd better agree to disagree on this subject."

"We're not finished with it," he said, "not by a long shot." Still he didn't press her anymore and gestured to the wicker chairs they were sitting on. "Zach made these himself. Collected the reeds, washed them and wove them into chairs."

Casey looked at the chairs with new interest. "He must've been very talented."

"He was."

She sighed tiredly and felt more than saw his scowl as he studied her.

"Look at you. You're exhausted," he accused.

"What was your first clue?" she asked, smiling.

He didn't return the smile. "Look around you. This old ruin of a place needs money, work and someone to put it to rights. Someone who knows what he's about."

"And you've looked me over and decided I don't measure up," Casey said, her good humor vanishing. "Well, let me tell you something, Mr. Reilly. I intend to live here and turn this old ruin, as you call it, into a home."

"Even assuming that you could fix up the house," he said, his tone indicating he thought she clearly could not, "what about the land? You can't even handle repairing fences. How're you going to clear the land? Haul away the junk that Zach had been collecting and storing for years? Do you have any idea at all how to make the land pay?"

Dragging a hand through his hair, he didn't wait for an answer. "Obviously not, or you wouldn't continue to let the prairie dogs destroy it. Why don't you admit you can't do the work, and sell out before it does you in? You're exhausted after stringing one fence."

"If this is such a ramshackle property, then why do you want it? You don't look like the kind of man who collects rundown houses and useless properties."

"I need this parcel of land to connect my two pieces of property. As it is, they're virtually cut off from one another. Adding this to our property would give us an uninterrupted range. Everything, from watering to roundup, would be simplified. I'd give you a fair price," he added. "More than market value."

Casey shook her head. "We don't have anywhere else to go. Such as it is, the house is mortgage-free. You probably don't have any idea of what it's like to worry about the rent due each month. I do, and believe me it's not pleasant." She stood. "Now, if you're finished, I won't keep you."

He stood, also, closing the gap between them. When the kiss came, she was too shocked to protest. It was hard and fast, as though he couldn't help himself.

Her hair tumbled about her face, and she stared up at him. "Why?" she whispered.

"I don't know," he admitted, looking no happier than she felt. Even so, his hands slipped to her shoulders, urging her closer.

She felt the warmth of his fingers seep through the thin cotton of her shirt, causing her to tremble with unexpected pleasure.

Conscious of his nearness and wary of her own reactions to it, she broke free. She backed away, anxious to widen the space between herself and Matt. Perhaps that would rid her of the breathlessness she was afraid was all too apparent to him.

Matt jammed his fists in his pockets. "I'll be seeing you."

She watched as he rode away and wondered why she wasn't angry. Anger, she understood. But the warm fluttery feeling in her stomach had nothing to do with anger.

Three

Casey rubbed the back of her neck and scowled at the coil of barbed wire. Her efforts at stringing fence today were proving no more effective than they had yesterday or the day before that. She shaded her eyes against the harsh glare of the sun to scan the field for Robbie. He'd gone exploring again but promised to stay in sight. A smile erased the scowl as she saw him running toward her.

"I brought you a present." Panting hard, he skidded to a stop in front of her.

Her smile widened as she took in the grubby hand clutching a bedraggled bouquet of dandelions. She knelt down to plant a kiss on his dirt-streaked cheek. "They're beautiful. Thank you."

"Do you really like them?"

"I love them. We'll use them for our table centerpiece tonight. Did you have a good time?"

"It was great." In the rapid change of subjects that only a six-year-old can manage, he asked in the next breath, "Can I help make dinner tonight? I'm a good hamburger-maker."

She laughed and ruffled his hair. "The best," she agreed. "And a pretty good hamburger-eater, too."

"Guess what I saw in the field behind the house?"

Her head swirled under yet another change of subject. "What?"

"A bunch of little animals. They look sorta like squirrels. Only they didn't live in trees like the squirrels back home. They were standing by little holes in the ground."

"Those are prairie dogs."

He shook his head. "Squirrels can't be dogs."

"These aren't *real* dogs," she explained. "Prairie dogs are like squirrels, only they live underneath the ground. Remember the little mounds we saw on the way to town?"

She took his hand. They tramped over the grass-tufted ground until they came to a cluster of small mounds of earth. "This is called a prairie-dog town." She pointed to the holes. "And those are the prairie dogs' homes."

Robbie pulled his hand free and squatted down to peer into the holes. "I can't see anything."

"They probably heard us coming and are hiding." She hunkered down beside him. "See the little marks around the holes?"

He nodded.

"Those are made by their noses."

He touched his own nose. "They put their noses in the dirt?"

Casey laughed. "Just about. They use their noses to push the dirt into a mound around the hole. That helps protect their home when it rains and also gives them a lookout place."

"What's a lookout place?"

"One prairie dog acts as a guard and keeps watch for other animals that might hurt his family and friends."

Her knees were becoming stiff, and she stood and pulled Robbie up with her. "I guess we scared them all off. Maybe we can see one another day."

"How come you know so much about prairie dogs?" Robbie asked as they trudged back to the house.

"I did some reading about them last night. A lot of people around here, like Matt Reilly, don't like prairie dogs. The ranchers want to get rid of them. I want to understand why."

"I'm going to learn to read in school."

She hugged him to her. "I know." Casey checked her watch. "It's five o'clock, and we haven't even started dinner! Race you home!"

She started running toward the house, but hung back to let Robbie outrun her, his short sturdy legs churning up the ground.

Robbie stopped abruptly. "Mom, look." He pointed at an approaching horse and rider.

Matt Reilly. What was he doing here?

"Good afternoon, Casey. Good to see you again, partner." He dismounted and put out his hand to Robbie.

Robbie reluctantly grasped it. "Hi, Matt." Though polite, the words lacked warmth.

Matt bent over and put his hand on Robbie's shoulder. "Something wrong?"

Robbie squirmed away. "Nothin'," he mumbled.

"I thought we were friends."

"Mom said you don't like the prairie dogs!" Robbie burst out.

Matt sighed heavily. "So that's it." He leveled a look at Casey.

"I just told him the truth," she defended herself. "Can you deny you think they're nuisances and want to get rid of them?"

"No, I can't."

Robbie turned an accusing glare at Matt. "I like prairie dogs. I don't like *you.*"

Matt squinted as he studied the late-afternoon sun. "I wish you did like me, Robbie, because I like you. I even like prairie dogs. But I also like cows and horses."

"So?"

"So sometimes what's good for one animal isn't good for others. In this case, the prairie dogs make the ground dangerous for the horses and cattle." He held out his hand. "Come on. I'll show you."

Robbie hesitated only a moment. Then he took the large tanned hand.

Matt waited for Casey to follow. ".You, too."

Reluctantly she joined them. They retraced the path she and Robbie had taken. When they came to the edge of the prairie-dog town, Matt stopped.

"Shh," he whispered. "If they hear us, they'll disappear into their holes." He crouched down.

Robbie followed his example. "See that big one?" Matt pointed to the buff-colored rodent that stood sentinel on the crest of his burrow.

Robbie nodded.

"He's the watchdog. When he senses danger, he'll warn his friends."

Casey squatted beside them. "He barks a warning," she explained.

"Not exactly a bark," Matt contradicted. "Wait—you'll see what I mean."

A prairie falcon swooped from the sky. The lookout gave a sound like a shrill whistle. Then he jumped into the air and bent backward so that his head nearly touched his rump. Immediately all the prairie dogs scurried into their burrows.

Matt stood and brushed the dust from his jeans. "That was a back flip. It's like when someone yells 'Fire' to us. It's the prairie dogs' way of signaling danger."

"Wow. That was neat." Robbie peered at the now empty field. "Will they come out again?"

"Probably not for a while, though a brave one may venture out a little later. They're pretty cautious and wait to make sure it's all clear before they leave their homes." Matt took Robbie's hand and led him carefully between the mounds of dirt. "All we can see are the holes. But underneath the ground there are tunnels connecting the holes

to each other. What do you suppose would happen if a
horse stepped in a hole?"

Robbie frowned. "Would he hurt his leg?"

"Probably. In fact he'd break it. When a horse breaks
a leg, sometimes he doesn't get better."

"Never?"

Matt exchanged a glance with Casey. "Most horses
don't recover from broken legs. Now can you see why
some of the other ranchers and I don't like prairie dogs on
our land?"

The frown furrowed deeper as Robbie thought on it.
"Yeah. But isn't there enough land for the prairie dogs *and*
horses?"

"That's a good question. One a lot of people have been
asking. But so far we haven't come up with an answer."
Matt slanted another look at Casey, who'd remained silent during the exchange. "What do you think?"

"I don't know," she admitted. "I guess I have the same
question Robbie has. Why *can't* we share the land?"

"Don't you think we've tried?" Matt hooked his
thumbs through his belt loops and rocked back on his
heels. "It's not black and white. Once you've been here
awhile, you'll understand. Maybe you ought to take a hard
look at both sides."

She looked up at the tall man regarding her quizzically.
"Maybe I ought to."

"Good." He threaded his fingers through his hair.
"Rob, I hope you'll try to understand, too. Sometimes it's
hard, but I think you're big enough to try."

Robbie expanded visibly under Matt's praise. "I'll try,
Matt."

"That's all I ask."

Robbie scampered off in front of them, heading to the
house, leaving Casey alone with Matt. They walked back
to where he'd left his horse, his arm draped around Casey's
shoulders. She willed herself not to react to the casual

gesture, but couldn't help the tiny frisson of pleasure that skittered down her spine.

"He's a good kid," Matt said.

"Yeah, he is. Thanks for what you said to him. Maybe someday he can understand most things have more than one side."

Matt nodded, about to speak when a rider, coming from the east, hailed them. "Hey, Matt!"

Casey looked at the sandy-haired woman and then at Matt. The resemblance was unmistakable.

"My sister, Lisa," Matt said.

Lisa Reilly dismounted with practiced ease. She walked over to join them. "Introduce me, Matt."

Her brother obliged and Lisa stuck out her hand.

Casey grasped it, not really surprised to find it almost as hard and callused as Matt's.

"I'm glad you're going to be living here, Mrs. Allen," Lisa said. "Zach's place has been empty too long."

"Thank you. And please, call me Casey."

"Casey it is, then. Matt told me we had a new neighbor. He didn't say much else, though." She chuckled. "I can see why—now."

Blushing, Casey turned to find Matt watching them, a frown creasing his forehead. Probably he disapproved of his sister's fraternizing with the enemy.

"I have to go," Matt said abruptly. "I'll see you later, Lisa." Then he turned to Casey. "Think about what I said. My offer still stands."

She watched as he mounted the big gray and rode off, his easy grace unsettling her.

Lisa regarded her quizzically. "What was all that about?"

"Your brother was lecturing me on prairie dogs. Seems he doesn't like them."

"Not many people around here do," Lisa agreed. "But that's not what he meant, was it?"

Casey shook her head. "He wants to buy me out. I refused."

"Oh, that," Lisa dismissed. "Matt's had that idea for years. But he wouldn't let it make any difference in how he treats you."

Casey chose her words carefully. "Perhaps you and he see things differently."

"Sure we do. Matt's ambitious and a hard worker. Me, I'm basically lazy. But I get things done. My own way."

Remembering the work-roughened hand, Casey doubted Lisa was lazy.

"You inherited this place from Zach Morrow?" Lisa asked.

"He was my mother's godfather."

"I'm sorry about old Zach, but I'm glad it brought you here." She grinned. "Matt mentioned a little boy?"

"My son, Robbie. He's wonderful. But I could be a little prejudiced." Casey smiled, thinking she was a *lot* prejudiced. "He'll be starting first grade tomorrow."

"This is a great place for kids." Without pausing for breath, Lisa added, "Come to dinner tomorrow night."

Surprised at the invitation, Casey hesitated. "I don't know, Lisa. There's Robbie, for one thing. And I'm not sure your brother would approve."

"Matt doesn't carry grudges," Lisa said confidently. "Besides, I make my own decisions. And Robbie's invited, too. How about it?"

"Dinner sounds wonderful," Casey said.

"Six be all right? Don't want to keep your little boy up past his bedtime."

"Perfect."

"Great. I'll see you then."

Casey watched her ride away. Maybe, just maybe, she'd found a friend.

Four

Casey savored the last bite of baked Alaska. "Delicious. Everything was, Lisa. Especially the steak."

Lisa looked pleased. "We raise the beef ourselves. Matt's always experimenting, trying to improve the herd. Make the meat leaner and still keep it tender."

"Does everyone around here ranch?"

"Just about. There're some farmers, too. Those who aren't ranchers or farmers sell supplies to them. We're all one big happy family."

"Except if you happen to like prairie dogs," Casey murmured.

"Hey, I *like* prairie dogs. I just don't like what they do to the land," Lisa said. "But forget about them right now. Tell me what you're doing to the house."

When Casey mentioned she planned to strip the kitchen cabinets the next day, Lisa immediately offered to help.

Lisa arrived just as Robbie left for school. She was dressed in jeans and a T-shirt that read, "Now that I've got it all together, what will I do with it?"

Armed with a scrub brush and an electric sander, she struck a comic pose. "Ready for orders, chief."

Casey burst out laughing. "Where did you find that shirt?"

"Matt had it especially made for me. He was always teasing me about the self-improvement courses I was forever taking. He said, very nastily I thought, that he couldn't see they'd done any good. I told him I had it all together. Hence, this."

"You and Matt are close?" It was half question, half statement.

"We've always been close. Of course, Matt's quite a bit older. Kind of raised me."

"He's a difficult person to know," Casey ventured.

"He is that," his sister agreed. "I think I know him, and then he does something that makes me realize I don't know him at all. There are so many parts to him. He's much more complex than I am." She shook her wire scrub brush at Casey in mock warning. "If you get me gabbing, we'll never get any work done. Lead me to it!"

Together they went inside. Lisa looked about in admiration. "You've accomplished wonders already. I remember it as very dark and depressing. It seems light and airy now."

"You're good for my morale. I did away with those heavy velvet curtains and hung plants in the windows."

They worked steadily for the next two hours. Slowly, a honey-toned birch appeared from under the layers of enamel that coated the kitchen cabinets.

"Why would anyone cover this with paint?" Casey wondered aloud. "You hardly ever see real wood anymore. It seems a shame to hide it."

"Zach Morrow was a strange old bird," Lisa said. "We never knew why he did half the things he did." She sighed, then changed the subject. "Hey, are you going to be coming to the town fair? I'm in charge this year." She pulled a face. "We're always trying to find new booths to raise money for a much-needed hospital. People get so tired of the same old thing year after year. I've got two weeks to come up with something that'll knock their socks off. Any ideas?"

"What about a portrait booth?" Casey suggested. "Perhaps a caricature one."

"That'd be great. We've never had anything like that before." Lisa frowned. "But we'd need an artist. One who was willing to work for free."

"I might be able to do it," Casey offered. "I've done a bit of caricature work before. It wouldn't cost much for the supplies. We'd need paper and charcoal. Pastels, if we want color."

"That's wonderful! To be able to draw, I mean." Lisa laughed. "Guess I'll just have to stick with my camera."

"Don't get the wrong idea. I'm not really a portrait artist. What I'm talking about are just quick impressions. Nothing fancy."

"All the better. We couldn't charge very much, but even so, we should make a nice profit." Lisa turned off her sander. "If I keep this up without a break soon, I'm going to start vibrating. Casey, I know we just met, but I feel like we're already friends. Matt's throwing a birthday party for me Friday night. Can you come?"

"You're sure I won't be barging in?"

"Are you kidding?" Lisa laughed. "Half the county will be there. Please say you'll come."

"It sounds great. I'd have to bring Robbie, though."

"No problem. We'll put him down in one of the bedrooms. He'll probably sleep through the whole thing."

Cleaning up after Lisa had gone, Casey wondered what she could get Lisa for a present. With no extra cash, she'd have to make something—perhaps a watercolor.

She was still puzzling over it when Robbie burst into the kitchen. She *thought* she'd heard the sound of the school bus a few minutes earlier.

"Hey, Mom!" he said excitedly. "Can I have a prairie dog for a pet?"

"A pet? I'm afraid not, honey."

"Why not?"

"Prairie dogs are wild animals. As cute as they are, they wouldn't make good pets." Seeing she wasn't getting through to him, she searched for an answer he could understand. "And they'd be unhappy away from their families and friends."

"I guess you're right. I was watching one just now when I got off the bus. He has a white tail. I named him Ralph."

"Ralph?"

"That's right. Ralph. Wanna see him?" He tugged at her hand, urging her to follow him.

She let him lead her to the field on the other side of the road.

"There he is!" Robbie whispered, pointing to a plump ginger-colored prairie dog cautiously peering out from his burrow.

"How can you tell that's Ralph? They all look the same to me."

"'Cause Ralph has a nicked ear. Look."

She stared hard and noticed the small slit in the rodent's right ear. "How did you ever see that?"

"I like to watch him. I saw him yesterday when I got off the bus. He's braver than the others."

"I see what you mean." Casey hunkered down and watched as the plucky little animal came out of his hole, looked around, then contentedly began chewing on a juicy thistle stalk. "But you know that Ralph wouldn't be happy living inside, don't you?"

Robbie nodded sadly. "Yeah." Then he brightened. "Could we come out here and watch him every day? That'd be almost as good."

She grinned at his enthusiasm. "I think we could manage that. Hey, what do you say to dinner?"

"I say yes!"

"You're going to be bigger than me soon," she teased.

"Even bigger," he boasted.

Four hours later, after she'd checked on Robbie, who'd fallen asleep halfway through his bedtime story, and cleaned up the kitchen, she sat at the kitchen table, the book on prairie dogs propped in front of her. With growing indignation, she read how some farmers had started exterminating prairie dogs with poison.

But, could she really blame them? Everything she read only confirmed what Matt had already told her. How could she defend the small animals, delightful as they were, when they threatened the livelihood of so many people?

She slammed the book shut and glared at it as if it were the cause of the headache that had been nagging at her all evening. She felt caught between two opposing forces, each good, each right in its own way.

"Oh, Zach. What have you gotten me into?"

"Lisa," Matt called. "Casey's here."

Radiant in a yellow halter-style dress, Lisa bounced into the spacious front hall. "I'm so glad you could make it," she said, her smile encompassing both Casey and Robbie.

"So am I," Casey said. "You look terrific." She handed Lisa her present.

Lisa opened it eagerly. "I can't wait. Matt says I'm like a kid at parties. Especially my own. But I do love surprises." She lifted the watercolor from its protective tissue and caught her breath. "It's beautiful, Casey. Did you paint it?"

Casey nodded. Instinctively her eyes sought Matt's, seeking his approval.

"You have quite a gift," he said quietly.

She wondered at the shadow in his eyes before Lisa leaned forward to kiss her cheek.

"Thank you very much," Lisa said. She pulled Casey into the room and introduced her and Robbie to everyone, showing off the watercolor as she did so. Robbie lit-

erally ate his way around the room, helping himself to all
the goodies Lisa had laid out. Casey smiled indulgently. It
wasn't often Robbie got to eat to his six-year-old heart's
content. After a while, between bites, he was yawning
hugely. Noticing it, Lisa said, "Come on, kiddo. Let's you
and me go find a nice room where you can have a nap."
She took his hand and led him, almost without protest, out
of the room.

Amazing, thought Lisa, how well her son took to the
Reillys. He seemed perfectly willing to do their bidding.
Her head spinning from meeting so many new people, she
decided to look for a quiet place to sit down.

She wandered out onto the patio and sank onto a wicker
couch. Digging a pencil and small sketch pad out of her
purse, she began to doodle. The lines took shape until a
familiar face smiled back at her. Even with the addition of
horns, Matt Reilly was unmistakable.

She stared at the paper, unbelieving. How had her doodling turned into Matt's handsome mocking face? Drat the
man. He was disturbing her thoughts, her dreams, and
now, even her art. She tore the paper off the pad, intend-
ing to throw it away. But then she stopped herself. Even
with the horns, it *was* a good likeness. In fact, the horns
lent it an interesting if somewhat sinister distinction. Casey
giggled. Did they reflect how she saw him? Ha! Wouldn't
an analyst have fun with that one.

Something blocked her light, and Casey looked up to see
the subject of her drawing. She gulped and hoped her face
didn't give her away. Casually she folded the paper in half
and started to slip it into her purse.

Matt sat down beside her. "May I see?"

"It's n-nothing. Only doodling."

"I'm sure even your doodles are beautiful." Gently he
took the picture from her fingers. Unfolding it, he paused,
then chuckled. "If all your caricatures are as successful as
this, you'll be the biggest money-maker at the fair."

"Please, Matt. I didn't mean..."

"You didn't mean to draw me or you didn't mean to draw me with horns?"

Fortunately Lisa appeared just then, balancing two plates piled high with delicacies. She handed one to Casey, then demanded, "What's wrong?" Without waiting for an answer, she turned to Matt and demanded, "What have you been doing to Casey? I can tell she's upset."

"Nothing," he said blandly. "She's been showing me an example of the caricatures she'll be doing at the fair." He handed Lisa the picture. "What do you think?"

Upon looking at the picture, Lisa burst out laughing. "Why don't we display this? It'd be great publicity for the fair and Casey's booth."

Appalled, Casey objected. "But people might think their pictures would have horns or something similar. And Matt might find it embarrassing."

"Oh, I wouldn't find it embarrassing at all," he said unhelpfully. "I think they make me look...distinguished."

"See?" Lisa said to Casey. "People will love it. Matt's so well-known. This'll advertise the fair in a spectacular way." She looked at Casey intently. "You don't mind, do you?"

"No, of course not," Casey lied weakly. When Lisa began to walk away, she glared at Matt. "It serves you right," she hissed.

He only grinned in a maddening way, seeming not at all put out. "Lisa," he called after his sister, "take care of that picture. It's the only portrait I'm likely to have of me."

"It's certainly the only *realistic* one you're likely to have," Casey muttered. "Any other artist would probably try to make you look pleasant—you'd be totally unrecognizable."

"You *are* in a mood, aren't you? Here, have some food." Before she could protest, he popped a meatball into her mouth.

Caught unaware, she almost choked on it. "I'll feed myself, thank you." She started to get up. "I'd better check on Robbie."

Grabbing her wrist, he forced her to stay seated. "Robbie's sound asleep. So there's no reason for you to run away."

"I'm not running away."

He raised his eyebrows.

"I'm not."

"No? Then stay and keep me company for a few minutes."

"I think I prefer more congenial company," she retorted, trying to twist her arm out of his grasp.

Matt's grip gentled. "I'm sorry. I shouldn't tease you. I'd really like your company."

She glanced at him uncertainly. "I don't know..."

"Good. Let's declare a truce. Deal?"

A smile edged the corners of her mouth upward. "Deal," she said, and put her hand in his.

He traced the fine network of veins visible beneath her skin. "You're trembling."

"No...I mean, it's a little cool." Immediately she regretted her lie, for Matt wrapped his arm around her, drawing her closer to him.

"Better?"

No! It was worse. Much worse. But she could hardly tell him that. "Yes, thank you."

"Sure?"

"Hadn't you better get back to your guests?" she asked, instead.

"I don't think I'll be missed." Leaning forward, he kissed her lightly. Unthinkingly, she returned the kiss, arching toward him. When Matt skimmed his knuckles along her cheek, she felt a dart of pleasure, entirely out of proportion to the simple caress.

When Matt drew away she took an unsteady breath and touched her lips experimentally. They were still warm. She stood. "I need to..." She turned and fled, thankful that he made no attempt to stop her, and walked straight into Lisa.

"Are you all right?" Lisa asked.

"Sure." Casey managed a small smile. "Why wouldn't I be?"

An unfamiliar voice interrupted. "Lisa, great party!"

"Thanks, Sam." Lisa turned to Casey to make the introductions. "Casey Allen, Sam Meacham. Another neighbor."

Sam Meacham's expression, friendly until now, hardened into an unwelcoming glare. "I hear you're camping out at Zach's place."

Casey nodded, puzzled by his sudden animosity. "It's our home now," she corrected.

"Rumor is you're as crazy as Zach, letting that vermin destroy the land."

"If you mean I'm letting a few animals make their home on my property, then yes, I am."

"Those animals are ruining good land for miles around." He wiped a beefy hand across his mouth. "Your land borders mine on the north. If one of my horses or cattle comes to grief on your land, I'll..."

"That'll be enough, Sam." Matt appeared suddenly. "Mrs. Allen just moved here. It's up to the rest of us to make her feel at home."

"Just as long as she knows the score." Sam Meacham stalked off.

Unconsciously Casey moved closer to Matt. "I'm sorry," she said, noticing the stares they'd attracted.

"I was just introducing Casey to Sam when he started in on her," Lisa said. "Gosh, I'm sorry, Casey."

"It's all right." She drew a shaky breath. "I guess I'm not too popular around here."

"Don't judge all of us on the basis of one man," Matt said. "Sam's not really such a bad guy. He's worried about his stock. We all are."

"I figured out that much by myself." She glanced around at the other guests. "Does everyone here feel the same way?"

He followed her gaze. "Some do. But not everyone. You have to realize that most of the people here make their living from the land in one way or another. It's only natural they want to protect it."

"I understand. I only wish they understood how I feel."

The reassuring words she'd hoped to hear didn't come.

Later at home as she helped Robbie undress for bed, Casey reflected on the evening. It had been an unsettling one, in more ways than one. Sam Meacham's venom could be dismissed more easily than her own instinctive turning toward Matt. How she had allowed that to happen, she didn't know. He aroused feelings in her she thought she'd buried with Dave. Sheer physical appeal, she could have handled. But it was more than that . . .

He was an attractive man. And a disturbing one. A dangerous combination. She'd do well to steer clear of him. Dave's long illness and death had left her too vulnerable to risk her heart again.

She concentrated on remembering that Matt was only interested in her property. Besides, he was probably no more interested in a relationship than she was.

Two sleepless hours later, she acknowledged she'd been lying to herself. She *would* do well to stay away from Matt Reilly. Not because he wanted her property. But because it would be all too easy to give him her heart.

Five

A week later, the day of the fair dawned clear and hot. Casey found herself as excited as Robbie, and not a little apprehensive at her part in it. She still agonized over the caricatures. Would people like the humorous drawings of themselves, or would they be offended by the sometimes unflattering exaggerations?

Her caricature of Matt, displayed in the hardware store, had received wide attention and publicity. She'd learned from Lisa that Matt had taken a great deal of good-natured kidding as to what had inspired such a rendition.

Casey had come in for her own share of teasing and curiosity. She'd parried the questions and speculations with a smile and shake of her head, unable to put into words her feelings about Matt, not even to herself.

"What are you thinking about?" Robbie asked as they drove to the fairground.

"I was just daydreaming," she said. "Grown-ups have dreams, too, you know."

"Do you like Matt?"

Casey let out a long breath. "Of course, I like him."

"Good," said Robbie. "So do I."

Preoccupied as she was, she almost missed her turnoff. Scores of people were milling about, setting up booths, laughing, sampling refreshments. Casey looked around in bewilderment, unsure of where her booth was and just what she should be doing.

She smiled in relief as Lisa approached, waving gaily. "Casey, thank goodness you're here! I've got a million things to do and no one to help."

At Casey's pointed look at all the people, Lisa laughed. "They're not here to help. Most are just here pretending to be a part of things. They're useless if you ask them to actually do something."

Casey saluted smartly. "What are your orders, Captain?"

Lisa ran her fingers through her hair. Stray wisps escaped their confining clasp. "Not captain. More like a drill sergeant."

At that moment, Matt joined them and took a hard look at Lisa. "How long have you been here?"

"Three hours."

"I thought so," he said, pushing her down onto a nearby chair. "Stay there. You won't be fit for anything if you don't take it easy."

"But the booths," she protested. "I need to show Casey where to go."

"*I'll* show Casey. You've done wonders, Lisa, but now it's time to let others have a chance."

She sank back. "You're right. It's just that I wanted everything to be perfect."

Matt turned to Casey. "Come on." He relieved her of her supplies. "I'll help you set up your booth." Taking her arm, he guided her and Robbie to the stall. She'd brought a small easel, a large tablet of heavy paper, and her pencils and pastels.

With a minimum of effort, Matt set up her easel and tacked up the poster she'd made to advertise her booth. Noting the exaggerated noses, eyebrows and ears that adorned it, he grinned at her. "No horns?"

She grinned back. "Only for those who've earned them."

Their exchange held no rancor now, only a shared amusement. She felt carefree and happy. "Do you think people will like these?" she asked, waving a hand to indicate the extravagant features.

"I wouldn't be surprised if your booth is the biggest draw we have."

She warmed at his words. To hide her pleasure, she busied herself arranging her equipment.

Robbie, who'd been remarkably silent until now, asked, "Will you do me, Mom?"

"Sure thing, Rob," Matt answered for her. "You can be the first customer."

Casey began to sketch her son quickly. Swift strokes outlined his face and put in angelic features. She chose to accentuate his freckles, which were, in reality, only the briefest dusting of gold, and his cowlick, which remained stubbornly erect.

Matt refrained from watching, and she silently thanked him for that. Satisfied with the caricature at last, she handed it to Robbie.

"Hey, it's me!" he said. "I look funny!"

"You're supposed to look funny," Matt said. "May I?" He held out his hand, and reluctantly she gave it to him.

Casey watched his expression anxiously as he studied the portrait.

He smiled. "It's perfect."

Lisa joined them and pounced upon the picture. "We should pin this up. It'll be a great advertisement for your booth."

Casey grinned, and Matt ruffled Robbie's hair. "All right with you, Rob, if we borrow your picture?"

"Sure. Where will you hang it?"

"I think at the fairground entrance," Matt said. "That way everyone will see it."

Pleased at their praise, Casey began to feel more confident. "I guess I'm ready for business."

"I wanted to be your first customer—" Lisa paused to smile at Robbie "—but I'll be the second, instead." She promptly sat down and struck an exaggerated pose. Casey and Matt exchanged glances, then Casey said with a pretended frown, "I don't know if I can do you, Lisa."

"Why not?"

"You're too perfect," Matt put in. "There's nothing to caricaturize."

Lisa pretended to preen herself, accepting this at face value. "Well, there is that, I suppose."

Matt hooted with laughter.

His sister poked him in the arm. "Ignore him, Casey," she instructed. "Just draw me as I am—beautiful."

Casey chose warm tones to highlight Lisa's golden coloring. Her initial hesitancy gone, she drew boldly and quickly. Lisa's ready smile appeared, her large eyes winked back at Casey. With increasing daring, Casey transformed Lisa's blond hair into a tawny mane, giving Lisa a catlike quality.

When she saw the portrait, Lisa clapped her hands in delight. "It's not what I expected at all. It's even better." She paid her money and carried it away to show off to everyone.

Casey's customers began to line up. Some approached her timidly, others cockily, with directions as to how they should be drawn. She merely smiled and drew what she felt. Everyone appeared satisfied, if surprised, with the results.

She worked steadily all day, stopping only when she needed to grab a bite to eat. Matt and Lisa took turns showing Robbie around the fair. And when the boy wasn't with them, he sat near his mother, fascinated like everyone else, by the work of her clever fingers. The money accumulated quickly.

When Lisa came to collect it at the end of the day, she gasped at the amount Casey had made. "I knew you'd do well—I just never dreamed *how* well," she said, giving Casey a quick hug. "You've brought in over five hundred dollars!"

Casey flushed in pleasure.

Matt joined them, hooking an arm casually around Casey's waist. "I think the artist deserves a reward."

"What kind of reward?"

"Are you game for a horseback ride, or are you too much of a city slicker?"

"City slicker? Them's fighting words," she said, trying to look fierce. "Of course, I'm game."

"Great. Be at my place at nine Monday morning."

That evening and all day Sunday, Casey pondered Matt's changed attitude toward her. Maybe, just maybe, he was beginning to feel something different for her. A smile tugged at her lips as she considered the possibility. Not that she could afford to get involved with anyone right now. Still, the idea persisted.

No longer did she feel as if he was trying to force her to sell her property to him. In fact, he'd been helpful and even concerned that she make a go of it. Had his feelings changed at the same time hers had? Or was he merely playing a game with her for reasons of his own?

No. She refused to believe it. Whatever Matt Reilly did would be straightforward and aboveboard. He could be a formidable enemy, but he would be an honest one.

The next morning, after she saw Robbie off to school, Casey was having second thoughts about her decision to go riding with Matt. She hadn't been riding in years, and that had only been on park trails.

Despite her misgivings, though, as she drove to his place, she was excited. This would be their day, one for her to look back upon and cherish. She arrived just as Matt was leading a bay mare from the barn.

"Are you ready?" he asked.

"As ready as I'm likely to be," Casey muttered, eyeing the mare warily.

"Come on," he teased. "You're not afraid of old Tess, are you? She's as gentle as a rocking horse."

"Rocking horses have been known to throw people."

Matt tethered Tess to the rail. "Just pet her, like you would a dog. She loves having her neck scratched."

Tentatively Casey stretched out a hand to stroke the mare's neck. Tess whinnied in pleasure. "Wow. She likes it." More boldly now, Casey stepped closer and stroked the mare's back.

"Of course she likes it. You two get acquainted while I get Jupiter." He disappeared into the barn. Minutes later, he led out his big gray gelding.

Casey kept a prudent distance from the animal. "You've seen Jupiter before." Matt said.

"I know. But we've never been formally introduced."

"I'll do it now," he offered.

"No, thanks. I think I'll keep our acquaintance to a nodding one."

Matt laughed. "Let me help you up." He checked the length of the stirrups and, satisfied, gave her a boost up onto Tess's back. He mounted Jupiter, whispering to him in a conspiratorial manner.

She could've sworn the big gray nodded in agreement.

Matt kept the pace slow, allowing her to adjust to the horse's motion.

A flock of Canada geese flew over them, their V-shaped formation resembling dark feather stitches embroidered across the pale blue sky. Prairie grass, bleached white by the sun, rustled under the mild breeze. She shielded her eyes against the brightness of the sun to stare into the distance, seeing the craggy peaks of the Rockies, already capped with snow.

"I can see why people never want to leave here," Casey said. "I wish I'd brought my sketch pad."

"Spoken like a true artist."

She thought she heard a strange bitterness behind the words and wondered at it. But before she could question him, he asked her about her work. "Do you do landscapes?"

"Not normally. I was a commercial artist before... before my husband died. I'd like to illustrate children's books someday."

"Why don't you?"

"It takes time to work up samples. But with Robbie in school full-time now, I plan to start updating my portfolio."

"You're good. More than good," Matt said. "Don't let your talent go to waste."

"Why do you care?" she asked before she could stop herself.

"I just do," he said roughly. "Even when I shouldn't." He didn't give her a chance to ask him what he meant, for he spurred Jupiter into a gallop.

More confident now, Casey tapped Tess lightly with her heels. The mare quickened her pace, but she was no match for Jupiter, who gave every appearance of being able to run forever. Casey gave a relieved sigh when she saw Matt pull Jupiter to a halt.

"Trying to get rid of us?" she asked when she caught up to him.

He pushed his hat back and swiped at his face with a kerchief. "Sorry."

"Did I say something wrong?"

"I had something on my mind."

His tone warned her off. The brightness of the day seeped away as she observed the grim lines bracketing his mouth, lines that hadn't been there earlier. Jupiter whinnied impatiently. Suddenly Matt smiled. "Jupiter's reminding me he doesn't like to be kept waiting."

The heaviness around her heart lifted at his smile, and she returned it. Matt seemed to have forgotten whatever had been troubling him.

As they rode, he told her stories about the area, some touching, others hilarious. He wove local legends into them, delighting her with his knowledge and love of the land. He painted pictures with his words so that she was actually seeing the brave men and women who had tamed the land and built new lives here.

She questioned him eagerly, especially interested in the pioneer women. He indulged her, recounting incidents of the strong women who worked, fought and died alongside their men.

Sometime later, they rode into a grove of cottonwoods that shaded a small lake.

"It's beautiful," Casey said. "Are we stopping here?"

"I thought you might like to." Matt dismounted, then helped her down. "Sore?" he asked, a wicked gleam turning his blue eyes gray.

She rubbed her backside experimentally. "Not too."

Matt grinned. "Let me know if you want a rubdown. I give great massages."

She ignored that.

He took a blanket out of his saddlebag and spread it on the ground, then unpacked the picnic basket. Fried chicken, potato salad, fresh peaches and thick wedges of chocolate cake appeared on the blanket.

Casey pretended to groan in dismay. "How many people were you planning to feed?"

"Just you and me. I know what a big appetite you have," he teased. "Of course, if you eat *too* much, you'll be too heavy for Tess to carry. So be careful."

She jabbed his arm, hard. He clutched it, moaning that she'd broken it.

Companionably, they munched on chicken, fighting good-naturedly over who got the last drumstick.

"I can see you as a pioneer wife," Matt said, returning to their earlier conversation.

"Why?"

"You have the spirit, the fire and the will to survive, all the things it must have taken in those times." His eyes were warm as they rested on her. "You remind me of my grandmother. She was a remarkable woman. Small like you, but with a fierce independence that drove my grandfather to distraction."

"I'd like to have known her," Casey said, pleased at the comparison.

"She'd have liked you. 'Give me spunk,' she used to say. 'Anything else is mere window dressing.'"

"Tell me more about her and your grandfather."

A reminiscent smile softened the normally hard lines of Matt's face. "They practically raised Lisa and me. We lived with them when my parents got divorced. My grandfather loved this." He waved his hand to indicate the expanse of prairie. "He'd say, 'Take care of the land and it'll take care of you.'" Matt's voice grew husky. "I've tried to build something he'd be proud of."

She pressed his hand. "I'm sure he would. You obviously loved your grandparents very much."

"We were closer than most kids and their parents are."

"Were they happy? Your grandparents?"

"They were the happiest couple I've ever known. And so much in love it almost hurt to see them together. Grandma said she and Grandpa were making 'memory days.' She told me that when I found someone special to build memory days with her."

Touched by the emotion in his voice, Casey felt the threat of tears in her eyes. "Not many have a chance to love and be loved like that. Having known love like that, it would be hard to settle for anything else.''

''Yes, it does make anything else seem pretty second-rate,'' he agreed. ''Did you and your husband have that?''

She didn't resent the question as she might once have. Somehow it seemed right that she should share that part of her life with Matt. ''Yes. Only it wasn't long enough,'' she said quietly, remembering the all too short years she'd had with Dave.

''Do you want to talk about it?''

She did. ''Dave and I were college sweethearts. We got married right after graduation, had Robbie a year later. Everything was going well—even his business had started to pick up. I was going to give up my job and try my hand at free-lancing. Then he started getting headaches.'' Her eyes closed as she remembered how their lives had been ripped apart.

''What was wrong?'' Matt asked gently.

''He had a brain tumor. The doctors said it was inoperable. When he . . . died, I was glad. Glad he didn't have to suffer anymore.''

''I'm sorry.''

Matt drew her into his arms, and she went willingly. She stayed there, needing comfort. But her feelings of comfort soon changed to something more, something less easily defined, something that caused her to pull away.

''How about you?'' she asked, wanting to turn the conversation away from herself. ''Isn't there someone special in your life?''

Matt didn't answer but lowered his head and brushed his lips against hers. Slowly he traced her lips with his tongue.

Casey knew a quiet joy at the pleasure his kiss evoked. She wanted to throw herself into his arms and bury her face against his neck, to breathe in the scent that was uniquely his. Suddenly aware of what she was doing, she pushed against his chest. Matt took the hint and dropped his hands. She noticed his breathing was not quite steady as he picked up an apple.

Her own breath came in ragged gasps. Desperately she searched for an answer to her behavior. Her husband had died two years ago. She was lonely. She would have responded to any attractive man.

But the rapid beating of her heart against her ribs made a lie of the explanation. It was not loneliness she was feeling. Far from it.

"Tell me about your parents," she said, determined to keep him talking. For when he was, he couldn't be doing other things. Things like kissing her, things like turning her inside out with needs she hardly remembered she had.

Until now.

Matt gave her a look that left little doubt that he saw through her ploy. "There's not much to tell. My mother's an artist. She had a showing at a gallery in Denver, had a bit of success and left to study in New York."

"Your mother's still alive?" She'd assumed both of his parents were dead.

He nodded. "She's working in Paris. At least she was the last time we heard from her."

"She never returned?"

"No." Matt's eyes took on a hard look. "She hates the ranch. Says it stifled her."

"When did she leave?"

"Twenty years ago."

She did some quick calculations. "You would have been fourteen then." What kind of woman left her children and never returned?

"Almost fifteen."

"And your dad?"

"Dad was a rancher, born and bred. The ranch was his life until he started letting it go downhill. He began drinking heavily, and it wasn't long before the booze killed him.

When he died, my grandfather ran the ranch until I was old enough to take over.''

"When was that?"

"When I graduated from college. I was twenty-one. My grandparents died shortly after that.''

He lifted his head to stare at the wide sweep of prairie.

She looked at him with new understanding. "You took care of Lisa and the ranch."

"She was pretty independent by then. Look, it was no big deal. I did what had to be done. Anyone would have done the same thing.''

"Not anyone," she contradicted softly. Bits and pieces began to come together. Matt's passionate defense of the land, his desire to unite the two pieces of family property. He'd had to grow up fast. Too fast.

"We'd better head back," he said abruptly. He began packing up the remains of their lunch.

She studied this complex man. Successful, dynamic, forceful, yet vulnerable enough to still hurt at his mother's desertion. Twenty years hadn't erased the pain. The dichotomy intrigued her, fascinated her, and scared her more than a little.

Silently she shook crumbs from the blanket and folded it before handing it to him. Just as silently, he tucked it into his saddlebag. He gave her a leg up onto Tess.

"Thanks," she said, and swung into the saddle.

The ride home held none of the morning's easy camaraderie. Casey was beginning to feel quite sore, and she held herself stiffly erect on Tess. The horse's motion, which had earlier felt like a gentle swaying, now became a jarring ride as Matt pushed them faster.

She was thankful when at last they arrived at the barn. She started to dismount, then hesitated, wondering how she was going to manage it. She looked uncertainly at the ground, which suddenly seemed awfully far away.

"Having trouble?" Matt asked. Before she could answer, he grasped her around the waist and swung her off the saddle and onto the ground.

She turned, acutely aware of his hands still resting on her waist, of the amusement in his eyes.

"Sore?"

If he laughs, I'll kill him. "A little."

"I've got some horse liniment in the barn. Works great on sore muscles."

"If you happen to be a horse. I think I'll pass." She smiled faintly, and the tension between them eased fractionally. Trying not to wobble, she led Tess toward the barn. Matt followed her and unsaddled first Jupiter and then Tess. He took a towel and began rubbing down the gelding. Tentatively, Casey copied his movements with Tess.

When they'd finished and returned the horses to their stalls, she said, "I ought to be going. Robbie will be home from school soon."

Matt didn't answer. Instead, he brushed his knuckles along her cheek. The simple gesture stirred her, and she fought to keep from swaying toward him.

When the kiss came, she was prepared. What she wasn't prepared for was the effect it had on her.

There was nothing tentative about this kiss, nothing tentative about Matt as he pulled her to him. With his hand cupping her neck and the other fitted against the small of her back, he held her still, his mouth roaming over hers, hungrily, possessively. Gently he lowered her to the earth floor of the barn.

Casey responded. She had little choice, with his body pressing against her own, his lips never breaking their contact. A soft moan escaped her lips. The hot heavy air of the barn, coupled with the pungent odor of horse and hay, only added to the tension building between them.

How long they stayed there, she couldn't have said.

When at last he released her, she rolled away from him, needing the distance between them. Her breath came in shallow gasps as she tried to understand what had happened.

Matt, too, looked stunned.

"We shouldn't have done that," she said.

He helped her up. "I won't apologize for kissing you. Given the same circumstances, I'd do it again."

She looked up at him. Was there regret in his eyes? Unspoken questions hung in the air.

He brushed a bit of hay from her hair.

She put her hands to her cheeks and felt their heat. Self-consciously, she picked the straw from her hair and then finger-combed it, wondering if he'd try to repeat the kiss. When he didn't, she didn't know if she was relieved or disappointed.

After she'd driven home, she tried to put what had happened into perspective. It was a kiss. A kiss between two adults who were attracted to each other. It was as simple as that.

Except she knew there was nothing simple about it.

Six

Water spurted from the shower faucet like a geyser. Convinced she'd lost her mind, Casey turned the faucet off, then on. Again, the water gushed out.

"Hey, Mom, you're all wet!" Robbie exclaimed.

"I know, isn't it wonderful?" She laughed and turned the water off.

"How come it works now?"

"I don't know, sweetheart. I'm only glad it does." For the rest of the day, she puzzled over the increased water pressure. Not one to complain about sudden good fortune, she accepted it, but still couldn't help wondering...

It wasn't until evening that she found the work order tucked behind, rather than inside, the trash can. A work order with Matt Reilly's signature on it.

Her anger grew as the truth sank in. Matt had arranged it. Because he'd felt sorry for her. The horseback ride had simply been a way to get her out of the house while he did his good deed for the day.

The next morning, after Robbie left for school, she drove to Matt's house. She'd worked herself into a fine temper by then. Who did he think he was, anyway? He had no business meddling in her affairs. She found him in his den and slapped the work order down on his desk.

He folded his arms and tipped his chair back. "Okay. So you know."

"Why?"

"Because I couldn't stand seeing you in that ram-shackle house with no water to speak of coming through the pipes. Did you even have enough water to shower, to wash the dishes, to do anything?"

"We had enough."

"When? Every other day? Every two days?"

Her chin lifted. "We were doing all right."

"Maybe I went about it the wrong way, but I did it because I wanted to help you."

She searched his face and, reading the sincerity there, felt instantly contrite. "I know. Only I don't want your charity. Can't you understand?"

"I'm sorry if I offended you, Casey. I never intended that. I guess I was out of line."

"You were. I'll pay you back as soon as I can. If I can sell some of my work—"

"I don't want your money. I want... Oh, forget it." He was already hunched back over his desk.

She stood there for a moment, then turned and left.

Conflicting feelings struggled for dominance as she drove home. She knew Matt had acted out of charity but, dammit, she didn't want charity. She wanted . . . What did she want? For him to look at her like a woman, not as someone to be pitied. What did someone like Matt Reilly know about struggling to make ends meet when the pay-check didn't stretch far enough to put food on the table and pay the rent? About the pride-killing experience of selling everything you had just to pay the bills? About the helplessness of watching someone you love die slowly, bit by agonizing bit?

She shook her head slowly. No, he wouldn't—couldn't—understand, no matter how hard he might try.

It was foolish, this wrenching feeling of closing a door on something special. For nothing had ever really existed between her and Matt. She still wasn't sure if he even liked her. He was physically attracted to her, nothing more. If she'd grown to care for him during these past weeks, she had no one to blame but herself. She'd known the risks involved. Now she must pay the penalty.

Casey sniffed, determined to put her feelings into perspective. Of course, she wasn't in love with him, she told herself. If nothing else, this should convince her they were light-years apart. She knew he meant well. But that didn't erase her sense of humiliation.

Two hours later, she pushed her chair back from the desk and glared at the drawing she'd been working on, acknowledging that her fit of temper wasn't helping any. The figures were stiff, their actions stilted. She wadded the paper up, adding it to the growing pile of trash on the floor. A knock at the door was a welcome distraction.

Matt stood there, the embarrassed expression on his face at odds with his usual self-assurance. "Can I come in?"

She hesitated, then shrugged. "Sure. Why not?"

He grimaced but followed her inside, closing the door behind him. "I came to apologize again."

"Oh?"

"You're not making this any easier."

"I didn't know I was supposed to."

"I'm sorry," he said.

The simplicity of his words touched her more than could any elaborate apology. "It's all right."

"No, it's not. I offended you. I could kick myself."

"I know." Strangely she did. Her anger faded as she realized how difficult this must be for him.

Clutching his hat awkwardly, he appeared more than a little uncomfortable.

"I suppose it's hard for someone like you to know what it's like," she said, wanting to put him at ease.

His mouth hardened, and she backed up. "What do you mean, 'someone like me?' " he demanded.

Aware that she'd blundered, she rushed on, "You know, someone who has everything . . ."

"You've got it all figured out, haven't you?" He jammed his hat on his head and turned on his heel.

Casey grabbed his arm. "I'm sorry. I didn't mean it that way."

He peeled her fingers from his arm. "How would you know what I have or haven't experienced?"

She shrank back at his tone. "I only meant—"

"I know what you meant. You think I was born with a silver spoon in my mouth." His lips twisted into a mirthless smile at the guilty expression in her eyes.

"You weren't?"

"Hardly. Mine has always been a working ranch. What I have, I worked for. And worked hard. Nothing was handed to me."

"I didn't mean that."

Matt took her hand and led her to the front porch. "See that?"

Not sure to what he referred, she shook her head. All she saw was the sun-washed prairie with its backdrop of mountains.

"The land. It can be a man's best friend or his worst enemy. If there's a drought two years in a row, a prairie fire or the price of beef goes down, it can cripple a working ranch. Most places around here are mortgaged to the hilt. I ought to know," he muttered more to himself than to her.

"Your ranch is mortgaged?"

"Not anymore. But when my grandfather took over, we were practically bankrupt."

"But your father—"

"After my mother left, my father drank and gambled away half the land. The rest he let go to waste. It took my grandfather six years just to pay off the bank loan. It took me another ten to buy back most of what my father had lost."

The land he'd tried to buy from her—was that part of what he'd lost? "I didn't know."

"Of course not. You're so hell-bent on making sure your pride isn't being trampled on you've got no time to listen. Maybe if you had, you'd know that around here we help each other. That's all I was trying to do. There's not a man or woman in these parts who wouldn't do the same."

"I didn't understand," she whispered.

He brushed the hair off her cheek. "Quit being such a hard case, and let me help you. Pride won't score you any points, not around here, anyway."

Ashamed, Casey looked down at her scuffed boots. "I'm sorry."

"Hey, it's all right." He fitted a finger under her chin and lifted it till her gaze met his. The warmth she found there unsettled her more than ever.

"Want to prove that I'm forgiven?"

She looked at him warily, and after a moment's hesitation, said, "Sure."

To her surprise he gestured at her desk. "Show me what you've been working on. I'd like to see it."

"Oh. All I've accomplished today is rubbish." She gestured at the pile of trash on the floor.

"Any luck in interesting a publisher?"

"A nibble from one, nothing definite. That's who I'm doing these for. So far I haven't been able to send him much." She bit her lip, not wanting Matt to guess *why* she hadn't sent other samples.

"Why not?"

She sighed, knowing there was no way she could avoid answering him. "Paper, paint. Unfortunately they cost a lot of money."

He frowned. "Why didn't you say something?"

She gave him a level look.

Matt held up his hands. "Okay. I get the message." He chucked her gently under the chin. "And next time, if you need help, call. That's what we do here, okay?"

"Okay."

"So I'd still like to see some of your work," he said. "Don't you have a portfolio?"

"An out-of-date one. The last couple of years…it hasn't been easy to work."

"Can I see what you're working on?"

"They're just sketches for children's books. I don't think you'd be interested."

"Try me." She disappeared into the kitchen, returning in a few minutes with her arms laden with sheaves of paper. Thumbing through them, she picked out the best. "I'm still working on them."

She watched as Matt studied the sketches. He paused over one of her favorites, a watercolor of a small boy fishing at a stream. The boy's eyes were closed, his fishing pole dangling from his hands.

"You're good. Really good. The publisher ought to beg you for more."

Her lips curved into a smile. "You're good for the ego."

He touched a finger to her lips. "I'd better be off, Casey. I just wanted to…clear the air between us." And with that he turned and left the house.

Through the window, Casey watched him mount his horse. As if aware of her gaze, he tipped his hat in her direction. She blushed a furious red and drew the curtains together.

"Mrs. Allen, I warned you. I warned Matt. Now it's gone and happened. I hope you're satisfied."

Casey stared at Sam Meacham in bewilderment. The rancher, astride a quarter horse, loomed over her menacingly. "What happened, Mr. Meacham?"

"Sheilah's broken her leg."

"I'm so sorry. How is she? Can I help? Is she in the hospital? Do you need someone to help with the children?"

He snorted rudely. "Hospital? Why'd she be in a hospital? She's in the barn, of course." He dismounted and stalked toward her, wiping his face with a sweat-stained bandanna.

Alarmed, she took a step backward and stared at him. "You put your wife in the barn?"

"My wife? Lady, you gone plumb crazy? Sheilah's my best mare. And a damn fine racer, too."

She sighed in relief. "Sheilah's just a horse. I'm so glad."

Meacham's face purpled, and a vein throbbed alarmingly in his neck. "Just a horse? Now I know you're crazy. My best horse's broken her leg and you're glad? You're some kind of vicious mean woman, all right, ain't you?"

"Mr. Meacham, I don't understand. You tell me Sheilah's broken her leg. I'm sorry about that, but I don't see what it has to do with me."

"It's those damn varmints you let run wild on your property. Well, they done broke down the ground so that a decent horse can't run on it without breaking its leg."

She gasped. Matt had warned her what might happen, but she'd been too stubborn to listen. Still, she didn't think she was solely at fault. "But if she was on your property, I don't see—"

"She weren't on my property. She knocked over one of *your* flimsy fences and got herself hurt on *your* property." He shot her a look of such righteous indignation she flinched.

"Mr. Meacham, I'm terribly sorry. If I can do anything—"

"You're darn right you can. You can pay the vet's bill. And if Sheilah doesn't recover, I'm suing you for everything you got. I'd planned on racing her, then breeding her. She won't be worth a plug nickel now."

"But it wasn't my fault..."

Meacham was already stomping away. "You heard me, ma'am," he called back over his shoulder. He climbed on his horse and glowered down at her. "You're as bad as old Zach. Worse. At least Zach was one of us. He belonged here. You got no business being here. No business at all."

Casey watched him ride away. "He won't go through with it," she told herself. "He can't hold me responsible." But even as she said the words, she knew she was lying to herself. Matt had warned her, and she'd refused to listen. *If Sheilah doesn't recover...* She shook her head, unable to complete the thought.

Shoulders drooping, she followed the path from the garden to the edge of the field. The prairie-dog town was alive with chirping rodents. One fat animal stood sentinel, posted at the crest of his small mound. A short whistle and back flip from him sent all his friends and relatives scurrying into their burrows.

How could such endearing creatures create so much havoc? She stood there for long minutes, trying to decide what to do. The burning rays of the late-afternoon sun persuaded her to head back to the cabin. She turned to retrace her steps, only to be confronted by the sight of another rider. The familiar figure dismounted and strode toward her.

Matt. She hadn't seen him for three days, not since he'd come over to 'clear the air.' She knew a cowardly impulse to run. The set of his shoulders, the grim lines bracketing his mouth, boded trouble. Instead, she stood her ground.

They measured each other, neither giving way.

She took the initiative. "Guess you heard about Mr. Meacham's horse."

"The whole county's heard by now." Matt pushed a hand through his hair. "I was afraid this would happen. Why didn't you listen?"

Stung at his tone and lack of understanding, Casey lashed out, her anger cutting through the apology she'd been about to make. "Because I couldn't let hundreds of animals be destroyed, that's why!"

"So, instead, you let another *valuable* animal be maimed? Do you know what usually happens to a horse with a broken leg?"

This time, she refused to meet his eyes.

"It's put down. Shot."

Her anger turned to horror. "But legs can mend. I read about a Kentucky Derby winner with a broken leg that healed."

"That was an exception. Sheilah has less than a fifty-fifty chance."

"I told Mr. Meacham I was sorry. I don't know what else to do." Her anger spent, she bowed her head. "I never meant to hurt anyone, let alone an innocent animal." She scuffed the toe of her boot at the tufts of prairie grass that dotted the ground.

"Look, Casey, I know you didn't mean for it to happen. I'm on my way over to Sam's now to see what I can do." His probing gaze didn't allow her to look away this time. "What I don't understand is why. Why do you keep defending these animals when you know the damage they do? It's not like they're an endangered species or anything."

For an answer she motioned him to follow her inside. She walked to the mantel and opened the brass box where she'd put Zach's letter. She handed it to him. Matt unfolded the paper and scanned its contents. He gave a low whistle. "So it was Zach's doing. I should have guessed. But you're not bound by this—legally or morally. You must know that."

"I don't want to see the prairie dogs killed any more than Zach did, but I'm beginning to see the other side of the problem, too. I just don't know what to do about it."

"I'll try to smooth things over with Sam. He's not a vindictive man. I think I can get him to see reason."

All at once Casey was weary. She didn't need another problem. And she didn't need—or want—charity from Matt or Sam Meacham, either. "Don't bother on my account," she snapped. "It's my problem and I'll handle it."

"Like you've already done." He reached out a conciliatory hand toward her, but she ignored it. "I'll talk to Sam, see if I can calm him down," he repeated. When she didn't answer, he muttered, "Be seeing you."

Casey stared after him, wanting to call him back and tell him she was sorry. He'd only come over to help, and she'd thrown it back in his face. All for the sake of pride.

Robbie would be home soon. In the meantime, she had to think.

Seven

Casey hadn't meant to eavesdrop at the hardware store several days later. She'd only stopped in to buy a few supplies, but she couldn't ignore the loud voices that filled the small space.

"Did you hear Sam Meacham's organizing a prairie-dog hunt? Seems he got real mad when his Sheilah took a fall in one of the holes. He's going all out—advertising, the works."

She stole a peek to see who was talking. A paunchy bald man in jeans and boots leaned against a counter talking to the clerk, Kyle Bridges.

"I hear he's thinking of advertising a reward for the man who shoots the most prairie dogs," Kyle put in.

"It'll sure help all us ranchers." The man gave Kyle a sly look. "Won't hurt you none, either. All those hunters in town shopping for supplies. Not to mention the tourists."

"You can bet I'm laying in a stock of ammunition."

The bald man shook his head admiringly. "You've got to hand it to Sam and Matt. I think they're really on to something."

"What's Matt got to do with it?"

"You kidding? Matt's as anxious to get rid of those varmints as the rest of us. They've given him plenty of grief, too."

Casey stood still, afraid if she moved she'd give herself away.

There must be some mistake! she thought. *As much as he dislikes the prairie dogs, Matt wouldn't be involved in anything like that.*

"You sure?" Kyle asked. "That doesn't sound like Matt."

I knew it!

The rancher pushed back his hat and glared at the clerk. "Sure I'm sure. Got it straight from Sam."

Pain welled up in Casey's throat, leaving a bitter taste in her mouth. She waited until the men's backs were turned before slipping out the door, her errand forgotten.

At home, she tried to summon some enthusiasm for varnishing the cabinets. Lisa would be here in a little while to help her. Chagrined, she remembered what she'd gone to the hardware store for—extra paint and brushes.

"You went to the store and forgot the brushes?" Lisa shook her head in mock disgust when she arrived a few minutes later. "They say the mind is the first thing to go."

"What? Oh, yeah." Casey smiled faintly. "Do you just want to forget it for today?"

"No way. We'll make do with the old brushes." Lisa began wiping down the cabinets with a clean cloth. After a while she gave Casey a stern look. "What is this? A one-woman operation?"

Casey flushed. "Sorry." She grabbed a rag and absently dragged it across the cabinet Lisa had just finished.

Lisa took the cloth from Casey and gently pushed her down in a chair. "Okay. What gives?"

"Nothing. I was just . . . Oh, it's nothing."

"Must be an awfully big nothing."

At Casey's silence, Lisa shook her head and said no more.

They worked silently, applying varnish, wiping away the excess. The repetitive motion suited Casey's mood.

Lisa looked critically at the newly gleaming wood. She pointed to the top edge of one cabinet. "I think you missed a spot. Up there. Don't bother," she said, as Casey started to drag a chair over. "I'll get it." Standing on tiptoe, she reached the unvarnished spot. "That's one advantage of being tall."

"Thanks, Lisa. I'd never have finished this by myself."

"That's what friends are for." Lisa stood back to admire their work. "If I do say so myself, I think we did one heck of a good job."

Forcing herself to match her friend's enthusiasm, Casey agreed. "The cabinets look great." Wearily she sank onto a chair, then realized she'd sat on something. "Yuck." She pulled the sticky brush away from her jeans, and to her horror her eyes filled with tears.

Noticing them, Lisa came over and touched her shoulder. "Come on, Casey, what's wrong? And don't tell me it's because you just sat on your paintbrush."

"Nothing's wrong. I just—"

Lisa planted her hands on her hips. "You've been dragging around like you just lost a winning lottery ticket." She gave a lopsided smile. "I've got a good shoulder to cry on."

Casey took a deep breath. "Have you heard anything about a prairie-dog shoot?" she asked, hoping it was all a mistake.

"Heard anything? It's all over town."

"I hear Sam Meacham is behind it."

"That's right. I heard Matt talking about it." Lisa paused as she swished the brushes in turpentine. "That's it, isn't it? You're upset about the hunt."

"Yeah, I am."

"But there's more, isn't there?" Lisa persisted. "I think it has to do with Matt, right? Not just the hunt."

Casey considered lying and knew she couldn't carry it off. "What else? Listen, could we talk about this later?"

"Sure." Lisa dried off the brushes. "Matt's my brother, but I know he can be an awful pain sometimes. My offer of a shoulder still stands."

"I'll remember." Much as she liked Lisa, Casey wanted to be alone and try to figure out what she was going to do. "Thanks again for your help."

Lisa grinned. "I can take a hint."

Casey tried to smile and failed miserably. "I'm sorry."

"It's all right. That's why we're friends."

Casey watched Lisa leave and knew a sudden desire to cry.

Two days later, she drove back to Little Falls. Another visit to the hardware store brought her face-to-face with the last person she wanted to see.

"Casey, we have to talk," Matt said, taking her arm.

"What about?"

Matt glanced about the crowded store, where curious eyes took in their every move. "I'd rather not do it here. Have lunch with me?"

She owed him that much. A tiny hope flickered in her heart. Maybe it was all a mistake. She would ask him about the prairie-dog hunt. He'd deny having a part in it, and...

She let him steer her to a nearby restaurant. When they were seated at a secluded booth in the back, Matt ordered. Neither of them spoke until after the waiter had reappeared and placed huge plates of steaming ribs before them.

Matt took her hand in his, ignoring her attempts to pull it away. "Look, I know you're upset about the prairie-dog hunt. That's what I want to talk to you about."

Please, say you had nothing to do with it, she silently begged.

"I think we can—"

"Did you talk with Sam Meacham about organizing this hunt?" she interrupted.

"I went to see Sam about Sheilah," Matt said, his tone cautious, his eyes wary. "I told you that."

That was no answer. "Did you discuss shooting the prairie dogs and selling tickets to it?"

"We talked about a lot of things."

"Did you or did you not talk about killing the prairie dogs?"

"Yes, we did," he said evenly, "but it wasn't the way you think."

So it was true. Her breath deserted her in a whoosh.

"I don't need to hear anything else you've got to say. I knew we didn't see things exactly the same way, but..." She swiped angrily at the tears that gathered in her eyes. "I didn't believe it. Not even when I heard it the fifth time. Everyone's so excited you'd think it was the Fourth of July, instead of mass murder."

"It's hardly murder."

"Oh. What would you call it? A bunch of hunters with their high-powered rifles shooting at defenseless animals?"

"You're not trying to understand the other side," Matt said, beginning to get riled. "This could mean a lot of money to businesses that might otherwise go under."

"And that's what counts, isn't it?" she asked contemptuously. "Money."

"You bet it counts. Businesses close up, people go hungry without it. You, of all people, ought to understand that."

Casey stood, her plate of ribs almost untouched.

Matt grabbed her hand, pulling her back down. "If you'll give me a chance to explain..."

His nearness threatened to shatter her composure. A day's growth of beard shadowed his face. The masculine scent of him tantalized her nostrils, further sidetracking her from her purpose.

She knew he was right and that she was being unfair. Still, she couldn't condone what he and Sam were planning.

"I don't want to fight with you about this," Matt said. "But neither can I turn my back on people who've been my friends for years. They think this could be good for the town, as well as making the land safe for our stock. I can't completely disagree with them. There might be another way, but don't—"

"I'm sorry, Matt. I know you have to do what you think is right. But so do I." She stood once more. This time he didn't try to stop her.

Casey walked out of the café, her head high. No one looking at her would know of the pain that wrapped itself around her heart.

At home, she flipped through the newspaper listlessly, trying to decide what she should do. An item on the editorial page caught her attention. Readers were invited to write their feelings about the proposed prairie-dog hunt. Two hours later, she looked over the paper she had just pulled from the typewriter. It was good, she decided. Before she could change her mind, she folded the letter into thirds, sealed it in an envelope and dropped it into the mailbox.

Two days later, Casey opened the newspaper to the editorial page with a mixture of anticipation and dread. Her letter was there. The paper had printed the entire thing. She drew a sharp breath as she read it. It sounded so much more vehement now than it had when she'd written it. A tremor of fear skittered down her spine. What would Matt think of it?

She found out soon enough.

The peremptory knock at the door could belong to no one else but Matt. Casey thought of ignoring it and decided she couldn't put it off. When she opened the door, he looked so grim and forbidding she involuntarily took a step backward.

He didn't wait for an invitation and walked inside, slamming the door behind him.

"Why? Why did you do it, Casey?" He waved the paper, folded open at the page of her editorial, at her. "It makes us sound like a bunch of bloodthirsty sadists."

"I'm sorry you see it that way. I only wrote what was happening. If you and your friends don't like it—"

"Don't like it? Every animal-protection agency in the state will pounce on this."

"I'm sorry," she repeated. "But I can't stand by and watch you and Sam Meacham stage a slaughter without trying to do something about it."

"If you'd only given me some time..."

"To do what?"

"To find a way out of this. Now you've gotten Sam and the others so mad they'll never back down."

"What makes you think they'd back down, anyway?"

"There's a chance. There *was* a chance," he corrected. "Do you think I want this? Do you?" His hands cupped her shoulders, and he shook her slightly.

Surprised by his intensity, she looked at him. "I don't know, Matt. I thought I did. One time. But now... I just don't know."

His anger spent, Matt dropped his hands. "I didn't want this contest, and not just because of you. I've never hunted. Never wanted to. This..." He waved his hands, then dropped them in defeat. "If you'd only waited. I was working on something that might have... Oh, what's the use?"

Exhaustion had deepened the fine lines that fanned outward from his eyes and furrowed grooves around his mouth.

Her gaze softened. "Why didn't you tell me you felt this way?"

"If you'll recall, I tried to,"

She recalled a lot more than that. She recalled the kisses they'd shared, the passion that erupted even when they fought. Most of all, she recalled the way he made her feel when he held her.

Matt gathered her to him, his arms closing around her. His mouth sought hers.

Casey moaned as she adapted to the hard demanding planes of his body. It was so simple, when they were like this.

After a few moments Matt drew back, and she felt bereft. "I'm sorry," she whispered. "I wish things could be different."

"So do I, sweetheart," he murmured, pulling her close once more. He rested his chin on the top of her head. "So do I." He sighed heavily. "I have to go. Maybe I can still do something about this mess." He turned and walked out of the house.

Bemused, she stood staring at the door, seeing not it but the tall, infinitely disturbing man who held her heart. She wanted to call him back, to promise anything if only he would stay.

When the letter from a local law firm arrived announcing Sam Meacham's suit against her, she wasn't surprised. The rancher hadn't left her in much doubt about his plans. Now she had to decide what to do about it.

She read further and blanched. Where was she supposed to come up with $100,000? She was still gnawing over the problem the following day while trying to fix another fence. When Sam Meacham drove up in a battered blue pickup, she resisted the urge to hide and made herself walk toward him.

He took one look at the fence she was repairing and muttered something about "a damn fool woman." Taking off his battered Stetson, he said, "I come to tell you something, ma'am."

"If it's about the lawsuit..."

"Sheilah's gonna be all right. That lawsuit was just me being ornery. Matt made me see it weren't right—suing you and all. That ain't why I'm here."

Relief mingled with a healthy dose of indignation. When was Matt going to learn that she could handle her own problems? "Why are you here then?"

"About the prairie-dog shoot..." He paused, shuffling from one foot to the other. "We called it off."

She hardly dared believe her ears. "You called it off. Why?"

He rubbed his hand across a whiskered jaw. "Well, it's like this. Matt and me got to talking about it. He said as how we'd have all those city folk breathing down our necks if we went through with it. We don't need a bunch of outsiders telling us how to run our town. And he promised..." He let his words trail off.

"What?" Casey prompted.

"Never you mind. Matt said he'd take care of things, and he will. The only thing you gotta know is there won't be no hunt." Sam gave her a fierce glare. "But that don't mean I like those vermin destroying the land."

"I know, Mr. Meacham. I'm trying to repair all the fences. It's just taking more time than I thought."

"Well, me and the boys are fixing to do something about that. Day after tomorrow. And, ma'am?"

"Yes?" she asked, still reeling from what he'd said.

"Don't you go messing with the fence anymore. You're a right pretty gal, but you can't string fence. And that's a fact."

Once she'd have taken offense at the criticism, but no longer. He was right. She couldn't string fence. "Thank you, Mr. Meacham. You're a nice man."

Bright color suffused his face as he glanced furtively around. "Don't go saying things like that. Someone might hear."

Automatically she lowered her voice. "It'll be our secret." She held out her hand and tried, unsuccessfully, to suppress a smile.

Reluctantly he took her hand and pressed it in his own callused one. Then he pushed his hat back on his head and headed toward his pickup.

"Mr. Meacham?" she called.

He turned impatiently. "Yes, ma'am?"

"Why didn't Matt tell me himself about the prairie-dog hunt being called off?"

Sam scratched behind his ear, looking suddenly uneasy. "Matt don't hold with a lot of jawin'." He slammed the door and started the engine. The pickup spit out dust as he drove away.

Casey watched him, her smile slowly fading. Once again, Matt had stepped in to solve her problems, first with persuading Sam to drop the suit and then seeing that the prairie-dog hunt was called off. Why couldn't he understand she didn't need someone to take care of her?

She just needed *him*.

She tried to focus on what was important. Both the lawsuit and the hunt had been canceled. She should have been happy. And she was, she assured herself. If only Matt had told her himself. If only he'd trusted her enough to believe she could take care of herself.

Eight

When the envelope appeared in the mail late one afternoon a week later, Casey held her breath. Recognizing the return address of the book publisher to whom she'd sent her work, she opened it with trembling fingers.

She read the letter, and with growing elation, read it a second time.

"They want me!" she shouted. "They want me!"

Ten minutes later, she was bundling Robbie into the car, intent on sharing her news with Matt. "But why do we have to go right now?" Robbie demanded. "I want—"

"Because." *Because I want to tell Matt and maybe, just maybe, he'll realize I don't need a caretaker.* Only him.

"Because why?"

"Because I'm excited and I want to share it with our friends. Okay?"

Her old car bounced over the rutted road, echoing the uneven rhythm of her heart as she thought about seeing Matt again.

At the house, Casey knocked, then waited impatiently.

"He's in the study," the housekeeper said. "Go right on in. Robbie and I can visit in the kitchen. I've got something for him."

Robbie's eyes widened in anticipation. Casey hesitated before tapping on the door, suddenly unsure of herself.

When Matt opened the door, his smile eased her nervousness.

"Matt, I heard from the publisher! He liked what I sent him for the book. He's talking about a multibook contract. Maybe." She paused for breath.

He grinned widely. "Sounds like you've got it made."

"He wants to meet me. In person." The words tumbled out. "Can you believe it?"

"Where *is* the publisher?"

"New York. Isn't that great? I've always wanted to go there. That's where most of the publishing houses are."

"Yeah. Great. When will you be leaving?" he asked tonelessly.

"As soon as possible." She gave him an impulsive hug. "I owe it all to you."

"I didn't have anything to do with it," he said, gently disentangling her arms. "You're the one with the talent."

"You encouraged me to try. Without that, I might never have had the courage to send in my work."

"Whatever you earn is because you have talent, Casey. Don't sell yourself short."

She fixed her gaze on him, puzzled. "Aren't you happy for me, Matt?"

He kissed her lightly. "Of course I am. Have you told Lisa?"

"Not yet."

"Why don't you go tell her now? She's in the barn. I'm sure she'll want to know."

"Okay." Casey backed away slowly. "Aren't you coming with me?"

"I'll be along in a few minutes. I have some things to finish up here."

Much of her excitement had dimmed, but she kept her smile in place. "Sure."

"Isn't it great, Matt?" Lisa demanded when he joined them in the barn fifteen minutes later.

"The greatest."

His smile didn't reach his eyes, Casey noticed uneasily.

"I've volunteered to keep Robbie while Casey's in New York," Lisa said. "Now, all we have to do is to get her some drop-dead clothes, and she's all set."

Casey waited expectantly for Matt to say something.

"It sounds as if you're all set," he said.

She saw Lisa throw Matt a curious look. "I'd better get going," Casey said. "It's late and I have to go home and make supper."

"Why don't you and Robbie stay here for supper?" Lisa protested. "We have to celebrate."

"Thanks, but I'd better not. Robbie needs an early night. And so do I. Thanks for listening to my big news."

She collected Robbie from the house, hoping as she did that there'd be some word from Matt. She quelled the impulse to go up to him and ask him what the matter was.

The ride home held none of her earlier exuberance. She listened to Robbie's chatter about all the things he was going to do with Lisa, but only added an occasional "hmm" in comment.

Later that evening, she wondered at Matt's reaction. She'd have sworn he was genuinely happy for her at first, but his mood had darkened with her announcement that she would be going to New York to meet with the publisher. Just over a week ago, he'd kissed her in a way that still left her reeling whenever she thought about it. Yet today... today he'd treated her like a stranger.

Perhaps she'd imagined it. She shook her head. No, for whatever reason, Matt hadn't been pleased. She hadn't realized how much she'd counted on his approval until now. His indifference cast a gray shadow over her happiness.

The following day, after Robbie left for school, she drove to Matt's home. She found him in the barn brushing down Jupiter.

She waited until he looked up from his task. "Hi," she said softly.

His lips slanted into a half smile. "Hi, yourself. What's up?"

She hesitated. "I wanted to thank you for getting Sam Meacham to call off the lawsuit. And the prairie-dog hunt."

"Don't thank me. It was Sam's idea. I just pointed out a few things to him."

"I wish you'd have let me handle it on my own, but," she rushed on when he would have objected, "I understand why you did it. And I'm grateful."

"Are you? I wonder." He turned his attention back to Jupiter.

She willed him to look at her, but he kept on with his task. "About yesterday. . . I wondered if I'd offended you or something . . ." Her voice trailed off uncertainly as she watched him.

He gave Jupiter an affectionate slap on the rump. "Why would you think that?"

"No reason, I guess. Only you seemed so distant." There, she'd said it. It was up to him now.

"Distant?"

She nodded unhappily.

"I've had a lot on my mind lately," he said.

"Then you're happy about my going to New York and everything? You don't mind?"

"Sure, I'm happy. Why wouldn't I be?"

Was he going to answer every question with a question? "I just wondered. That's all." *How lame can you get, Casey?*

"You're happy, aren't you?" He looked at her keenly. "A chance to illustrate children's books. A dream come true."

"Yes, but maybe I shouldn't go. Not yet, anyway. I plan to leave in five days, but Robbie's just getting settled and—"

"Not go? And give up this chance?" He covered the few feet separating them. Framing her face with his hands, he said, "Of course, you should go. I'll be rooting for you. We all will."

Her smile trembled around the edges, but she managed to keep it in place. "Thanks."

He dropped his hands. "Look, you'd better run along now. I know you must have a lot to do."

She paled at the brusqueness of his voice.

"And I've got a lot of work, too." He gestured at the leather soap and pile of tack.

"Will I see you tomorrow?" she asked.

"Probably not. I've got to go out of town. I won't be back for a few days."

"Oh. Well, I'll see you before I go, won't I?"

Already bent over the tack, he shook his head. "I'm going to be pretty busy. Have a good trip."

"Sure." She backed out of the barn, hoping he'd look up and say something. Anything.

Somehow, she managed to get out of the house and into her car before humiliating herself further. She wouldn't waste another tear on him, she vowed.

The lone tear that trailed down her cheek didn't count.

She'd promised to meet Lisa in town to do some shopping. Any other time, she'd have been thrilled at the chance to buy new clothes. But now, she could barely rouse the energy to try on the dresses Lisa handed her.

She sensed Lisa's puzzlement but didn't try to excuse her lack of enthusiasm. How could she explain to Lisa what she didn't understand herself?

Trying to muster some excitement for the trip to New York, Casey spent the rest of the afternoon in her bedroom, putting away the new clothes she and Lisa had bought, but the colors blurred before her eyes. A silky peach dress slipped through her fingers. Would Matt like it?

Angrily she snatched the dress from where it'd fallen to the floor and crammed it into the closet. If Matt didn't care, well, that was just too bad. The opportunity to show a publisher more of her work was a chance in a million. It was everything she'd been working toward. If she didn't grab it, she might not get another chance. She had to take it.

So why did she feel like crying? She didn't have to look far for the answer.

Matt had made it clear he wasn't interested. She'd given him every chance to tell her he cared. A sob caught in her throat as she remembered his indifference this morning.

Suddenly she had a change of plans. She'd take Robbie with her to New York. They wouldn't come back. Even the uncertainty of finding a place there and starting all over again couldn't sway her from her decision. She couldn't bear to be that close to Matt, knowing he didn't return her love.

Reluctantly she told Lisa of her plans when Matt's sister came over the next day.

"I didn't mean it to happen," she said, trying to explain her feelings for Matt. "When I realized what was happening, I even tried to dislike him. But it didn't work."

Lisa looked at Casey with compassionate eyes. "We can't always love to order. Are you sure about Matt? About how he feels, I mean?"

Casey nodded miserably. "He made it pretty clear."

Lisa swore under her breath. "That brother of mine needs a swift kick."

"Will you help me settle things here?"

"Leave everything to me. You're sure you want to sell the house?"

Casey nodded.

"All right," Lisa said. "I guess Matt'll be pleased. He's wanted this property for a long time."

"Lisa," said Casey, "I don't want him to know I'm selling. At least not yet. Not until Robbie and I are good and gone. Okay?"

Lisa nodded and said reluctantly, "Okay, but—"

"No buts," said Casey. "It's better that way." She paused. "There's one thing, though." She paused. "The prairie dogs..."

"Sam Meacham dropped his suit, didn't he?" Lisa asked.

"Yeah. Once Sheilah recovered. He also told me he'd decided not to go through with the shoot and even offered to repair my fences."

"What's the problem, then?"

"I still feel responsible for the animals on Zach's land."

"I won't let them be destroyed," Lisa promised. "I don't know how, but I'll figure out something."

Impulsively Casey hugged her. "I'll never have a better friend than you." Then a frown pleated her brow. "I hate having to ask you to deceive Matt but it won't be for long. He'll be pleased in the end, finally getting his land."

"Yeah, guess so." Lisa didn't sound convinced. "He's away this weekend, so this'll be your chance. Can you and Robbie be ready to leave in two days?"

"I'll be ready," Casey said. "Oh, Lisa, I don't want to go."

"Stay, then," Lisa urged. "Maybe things will work out between you and Matt if you give it more time."

Casey's expression stiffened with resolve. "No. I'd only be kidding myself. You've been a terrific friend, Lisa. I'll never forget you. Or be able to repay you."

Lisa sniffed and wiped her eyes. "If you don't stop, you'll have me bawling like a baby."

"Mom, can we say goodbye to Ralph?" Robbie asked as Lisa helped them load their suitcases into the car Saturday morning.

Casey checked her watch, impatient to be on their way. One look at Robbie's face convinced her a few minutes wouldn't matter.

"Sure we can."

They tramped through the pocked field. While Robbie scampered off to find Ralph, she looked at the rugged landscape, now gilded a burnished brown under the autumn sun. Though some wouldn't find it beautiful, it was to her.

Would they find another place they could call home?

Nine

Casey caught sight of a highway-patrol car in the rearview mirror. Its driver seemed to be motioning her to pull over. Puzzled, she did as directed.

"Ma'am, I have orders to detain you," the boyish-looking officer said.

Fumbling for her license and registration, she missed the hint of a smile in his eyes.

"I don't understand, officer. Have I done something wrong?"

"If you'll just follow me," he said pleasantly.

Feeling she had no choice, Casey nodded. Robbie, who despite the constraints of his seat belt had managed to doze off, looked up and sleepily rubbed his eyes.

"Mom, why are we stopped?"

"We need to follow that policeman." She pointed to the uniformed man and started the car.

Excited at the prospect of meeting a real policeman, Robbie seemed to forget his sadness about leaving. "Are we being arrested? Were you speeding? Will we go to jail? Will they take our fingerprints?"

"I don't know!" she said, frustrated at the delay and concerned about what it might mean. Robbie's questions died away at her abrupt reply. He looked down at his hands. "I'm sorry," he said in a small voice.

Contritely she placed her hand on his. "No, Robbie. I'm the one who's sorry. I shouldn't have snapped at you like that. I guess I'm a little nervous."

"It's all right, Mom. I'll take care of you."

She smiled at that, touched by the seriousness of his reply. "I know you will, honey."

Up ahead, she could see the substation of the highway patrol. She pulled in alongside the patrol car.

The boyish officer held the door open, motioning for her and Robbie to go inside. Robbie clung to her hand, whether in reassurance or fear, she wasn't sure. Indicating chairs for them, the officer then held a whispered consultation with his sergeant, making frequent gestures toward herself.

Casey's anxiety mounted steadily; her grip on Robbie's hand tightened until he tugged it away.

"Mom, you're hurting me," he complained.

"I'm sorry, Robbie," she apologized in a low voice. "I can't imagine what they want with us."

Finally the sergeant approached them, smiling broadly. "Mrs. Allen, please come with me." Casey didn't immediately stand up. She glanced at Robbie.

Interpreting her hesitation correctly, the sergeant reassured her. "There's no cause for alarm. And this young man here—" he smiled at Robbie "—can stay with Officer McBride." He pointed at the young officer who had escorted them there.

The sergeant ushered her into an office marked Private. To her surprise, he didn't remain but backed quickly out, closing the door behind him.

No one sat at the room's solitary desk and at first it appeared empty. A movement at the far corner caught her attention.

"No," she whispered.

Looking exceedingly grim, Matt walked toward her. With nowhere to run and unable to take her eyes from him, Casey remained still.

He stopped several feet short of her. His eyes were bloodshot, his skin gray, and his clothes looked as if he'd slept in them. And she wanted nothing more than to hurl herself into his arms and feel his lips on hers.

Instead, she asked in what she hoped was a calm voice, "You had me brought here?" She didn't wait for him to answer. "Why? And how?"

"The sergeant's an old friend," Matt explained. "He put out your description and license number in a one-hundred-mile radius."

"That's illegal to track me down that way."

"A little," he admitted.

"You're not supposed to be here," she said. "You're on a business trip."

"Obviously I'm not. I got as far as the airport and found I couldn't leave. I came back to try..." He closed the remaining distance between them, and she found herself in his arms, his lips pressed against her own.

"Where were you going, anyway?" she asked when he lifted his mouth.

"Salt Lake City."

"I didn't know you had any business there."

"I don't. It's in Provo."

"Provo?"

"I've been corresponding with a Dr. Jeffers at Brigham Young University. He's an expert on the transplantation of wild animals."

Understanding wreathed her face in smiles. "The prairie dogs. We can relocate their towns."

He nodded. "I've been investigating a way to save them and at the same time make the land safe for the cattle and horses. I found a professor at BYU who's done research on the subject of transplanting prairie dogs. It can be done. It takes time and money, but it works."

"That's where you went two weeks ago?" she guessed. "Why didn't you tell me?"

"I wanted to."

"But why didn't you?"

"A couple of reasons. One, I wasn't sure if you'd like it."

Her brow scrunched into a frown. "Why wouldn't I like it?"

"You're familiar with the concept of balance of nature?"

"You mean, where the animal population takes care of itself?"

He nodded, watching her expression. "The prairie dogs will become part of that balance, along with the other animals that occupy the land."

She swallowed, knowing they would become the prey of hawks, coyotes and snakes. "It sounds like a good plan."

"Even when it means all the prairie dogs won't survive?"

She managed a shaky nod. "What was the second reason you couldn't tell me about this?"

He smiled slightly. "If you remember, you didn't listen much. I wanted to be sure before I talked to you. And I didn't want your gratitude."

"Why not?"

"Because I wanted something much more important."

"What?" she asked, hardly daring to hope.

He barely hesitated. "Your love."

"You have that. You've always had that."

"I couldn't be sure . . ." His thumb massaged the nape of her neck, destroying any power of thought she might possess. "Why did you leave, Casey?"

She tried to pull away from him, but he only tightened his hold on her. "I'm going to New York, remember?"

"You were taking everything with you. Including Robbie. That doesn't sound like a short trip. I want the truth."

"I was leaving."

"For good?"

She nodded.

"Why?"

She pretended an interest in the calendar on the wall. "I decided it was too good of an opportunity to pass up. Robbie will get to see New York, I'll have time to meet other publishers, and we can do some sight-seeing. If things work out, we might even settle there permanently."

"What about us?" he demanded, tilting her chin so that their eyes met.

"What about us?" she echoed.

"You were leaving without saying goodbye."

"We said our goodbyes, remember?"

"I remember acting like a fool. I also remember wanting to do this." He kissed her again. "And this." He undid the top button of her blouse to place a kiss on the sensitive hollow of her throat.

"I thought you didn't care," she said when talking became possible again. "I couldn't bear to be that close to you and know you didn't . . ."

"Didn't what?"

"Didn't love me," she mumbled against his chest. Even as she said the words, they caught in her throat.

"And that matters to you?"

She nodded.

"Look at me," he said. "I love you. Love you so much it scares me. I tried to let you go, but found I couldn't."

"Why? Why did you try to let me go?"

"So you could go to New York and have the career you wanted. You deserve a chance at making your dreams come true."

"Everything I've ever wanted is here. You. Robbie. Nothing else matters."

"What about your work?"

She read the doubt in his eyes and ached for the teenage boy who'd never fully recovered from his mother's rejection.

Matt looked away. "My mother accused my father of wanting to hold her back. She said her career never got off the ground because of her family. She wanted acknowledgment of her work, recognition from the art world."

"She didn't get it?"

His lips twisted. "You could say that. After her first success, she was ignored. She blamed everyone and everything, everything except the fact that she couldn't cut it. Finally she left."

"And you're afraid I'll be the same."

"No. I *know* you're good. So good you're going to make it. I didn't want to stand in your way. I didn't want that for you—for us. I love you too much."

His admission humbled her. "And I love you. Don't you know you're more important than any job? The publisher wants me to illustrate a picture book. Maybe even a whole series of books if things work out right, but none of that matters if it means I'd lose you."

"You won't lose me. But I know how important your work is to you. Could you be happy here? We don't have book publishers or anything else that a city like New York can offer. And we aren't likely to, either."

"Those things don't make a home. It's the people you're with that count." She hesitated. "I still have to go to New York and settle things."

"Not without me, you don't."

"I was hoping you'd say that," she said, a smile hovering on her lips. The smile faded as she realized how close she'd come to losing him. "I can illustrate books anywhere, but without you, it doesn't matter."

"I know." Shivers danced along her spine at the huskiness of his voice. "I feel the same way." He proved his words by kissing her, lightly at first, and then more deeply.

"What made you come after me?" she asked.

He grimaced and rubbed his jaw. "Lisa told me a few home truths. Things I would've figured out for myself if I hadn't been acting like a jackass. I want to make memory days with you, Casey. I want a whole passel of memory days. I've been thinking of turning the back porch into a studio. It's got plenty of light and..."

She kissed him. "I love you. But I wouldn't care if we lived in a shack, as long as we're together."

"Are you asking me to marry you?" he said.

"I was trying to."

He groaned and tightened his hold on her. "You little wretch. You put me through agonies."

"And what about me? Sometimes I felt as if you didn't even like me."

"'Like' has always been too tame a word for what I feel for you." His mouth claimed hers again, effectively silencing her.

Her hands reached up to twine around his neck. "It's all right now. Nothing matters now that we're together." Casey snuggled against him and turned up her face for another kiss.

His lips brushed hers, their touch a promise for today and all the tomorrows that followed.

Suddenly she pulled away and looked up at him. "About Robbie..."

Matt smiled. "I'll start investigating how to go about adopting him, if that's okay with you. He'll be the start of our family. He'll make a good big brother for our other children."

"Our other children?"

"At least one of each. With red curls and brown eyes like their mother."

"No," she contradicted. "They'll have brown hair and blue eyes like their father."

"Are you going to start arguing with me already?"

She shook her head. "I'll wait until after we're married." Her voice caught. "I love you so much it hurts."

"Not half as much as I love you."

A rap at the door interrupted what she'd been about to say. Officer McBride gave them an apologetic look. "Sorry to bother you, ma'am, sir, but this young fellow is feeling a mite lonely."

Robbie bounded into the room, took in the situation and grinned hugely. "Hey, Mom, Matt, I wanna go home!"

Casey and Matt exchanged smiles and drew apart. Matt took Robbie's hand. "I guess we'd better get used to this."

Casey watched them together, the small boy holding the big man's hand. Love had come, unexpectedly, wonderfully, in its own time.

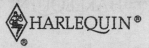

HARLEQUIN®

**COMING SOON TO
A STORE NEAR YOU...**

THE MAIN ATTRACTION

By *New York Times* Bestselling Author

This March, look for THE MAIN ATTRACTION by popular
author Jayne Ann Krentz.

Ten years ago, Filomena Cromwell had left her small town
in shame. Now she is back determined to get her sweet,
sweet revenge....

Soon she has her ex-fiancé, who cheated on her with
another woman, chasing her all over town. And he isn't
the only one. Filomena lets Trent Ravinder catch her.

Can she control the fireworks she's set into motion?

BOB8

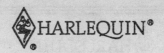

HARLEQUIN®

MARRIAGE BY Design

Harlequin proudly presents four stories about *convenient* but not *conventional* reasons for marriage:

- ◆ To save your godchildren from a "wicked stepmother"

- ◆ To help out your eccentric aunt—and her sexy business partner

- ◆ To bring an old man happiness by making him a grandfather

- ◆ To escape from a ghostly existence and become a real woman

Marriage By Design—four brand-new stories by four of Harlequin's most popular authors:

CATHY GILLEN THACKER
JASMINE CRESSWELL
GLENDA SANDERS
MARGARET CHITTENDEN

Don't miss this exciting collection of stories about marriages of convenience. Available in April, wherever Harlequin books are sold.

MBD94

Fifty red-blooded, white-hot, true-blue hunks
from every State in the Union!

Look for MEN MADE IN AMERICA! Written by some of
our most popular authors, these stories feature fifty of
the strongest, sexiest men, each from a different state in
the union!

Two titles available every other month at your favorite
retail outlet.

In March, look for:

TANGLED LIES by Anne Stuart (Hawaii)
ROGUE'S VALLEY by Kathleen Creighton (Idaho)

In April, look for:

LOVE BY PROXY by Diana Palmer (Illinois)
POSSIBLES by Lass Small (Indiana)

You won't be able to resist MEN MADE IN AMERICA!

Where do you find hot Texas nights, smooth Texas charm and dangerously sexy cowboys?

Crystal Creek reverberates with the exciting rhythm of Texas. Each story features the rugged individuals who live and love in the Lone Star State.

"...Crystal Creek wonderfully evokes the hot days and steamy nights of a small Texas community."   —*Romantic Times*

"...a series that should hook any romance reader. Outstanding."
                                                          —*Rendezvous*

"Altogether, it couldn't be better."   —*Rendezvous*

Don't miss the next nook in this exciting series.
PASSIONATE KISSES by PENNY RICHARDS

Available in April wherever Harlequin books are sold.

CC14

Harlequin® Historical

LOOK TO THE PAST FOR FUTURE FUN AND EXCITEMENT!

The past the Harlequin Historical way, that is. 1994 is going to be a banner year for us, so here's a preview of what to expect:

* The continuation of our bigger book program, with titles such as *Across Time* by Nina Beaumont, *Defy the Eagle* by Lynn Bartlett and *Unicorn Bride* by Claire Delacroix.

* A 1994 March Madness promotion featuring four titles by promising new authors Gayle Wilson, Cheryl St. John, Madris Dupree and Emily French.

* Brand-new in-line series: DESTINY'S WOMEN by Merline Lovelace and HIGHLANDER by Ruth Langan; and new chapters in old favorites, such as the SPARHAWK saga by Miranda Jarrett and the WARRIOR series by Margaret Moore.

* *Promised Brides,* an exciting brand-new anthology with stories by Mary Jo Putney, Kristin James and Julie Tetel.

* Our perennial favorite, the Christmas anthology, this year featuring Patricia Gardner Evans, Kathleen Eagle, Elaine Barbieri and Margaret Moore.

Watch for these programs and titles wherever Harlequin Historicals are sold.

HARLEQUIN HISTORICALS...
A TOUCH OF MAGIC!

HHPROM094

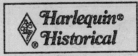

Harlequin® Historical

Looking for more of a good thing?

Why not try a bigger book from Harlequin Historicals?

SUSPICION by Judith McWilliams, April 1994—A story of intrigue and deceit set during the Regency era.

ROYAL HARLOT by Lucy Gordon, May 1994—The adventuresome romance of a prince and the woman spy assigned to protect him.

UNICORN BRIDE by Claire Delacroix, June 1994—The first of a trilogy set in thirteenth-century France.

MARIAH'S PRIZE by Miranda Jarrett, July 1994—Another tale of the seafaring Sparhawks of Rhode Island.

Longer stories by some of your favorite authors. Watch for them this spring, wherever Harlequin Historicals are sold.